"COUNT ON SASH...
FIRST-RATE, BLIS...
—Suzanne McMinn, au...

PRAISE FOR THE NOVELS OF SASHA WHITE

"The writing is strong, the characterization is well drawn and likable . . . and the sex is very well done. This is *hot!*"

—Angela Knight

"Torrid . . . [a] sheet burner."

"Plenty of fun . . . mixes tense emo...

"Packs a tremendous punch . . . stimulating, steamy, [and] scorching hot."   —*Fallen Angel Reviews*

"Hot, fast paced, and erotic."   —*Romance Divas*

"Hot and explosive."   —*Just Erotic Romance Reviews*

"Intensely sensual."   —*Romance Junkies*

"Creates a carnal haze that envelops the readers, caresses their senses . . . deliciously decadent."   —*The Romance Studio*

"Soul grabbing, richly evocative, and unforgettable."
—Suzanne McMinn

"Sexy, raw, and intriguing."   —*The Road to Romance*

WICKED

SASHA WHITE

HEAT
NEW YORK, NEW YORK

THE BERKLEY PUBLISHING GROUP
Published by the Penguin Group
Penguin Group (USA) Inc.
375 Hudson Street, New York, New York 10014, USA
Penguin Group (Canada), 90 Eglinton Avenue East, Suite 700, Toronto, Ontario M4P 2Y3, Canada
(a division of Pearson Penguin Canada Inc.)
Penguin Books Ltd., 80 Strand, London WC2R 0RL, England
Penguin Group Ireland, 25 St. Stephen's Green, Dublin 2, Ireland (a division of Penguin Books Ltd.)
Penguin Group (Australia), 250 Camberwell Road, Camberwell, Victoria 3124, Australia
(a division of Pearson Australia Group Pty. Ltd.)
Penguin Books India Pvt. Ltd., 11 Community Centre, Panchsheel Park, New Delhi—110 017, India
Penguin Group (NZ), 67 Apollo Drive, Rosedale, North Shore 0632, New Zealand
(a division of Pearson New Zealand Ltd.)
Penguin Books (South Africa) (Pty.) Ltd., 24 Sturdee Avenue, Rosebank, Johannesburg 2196, South Africa

Penguin Books Ltd., Registered Offices: 80 Strand, London WC2R 0RL, England

This is an original publication of The Berkley Publishing Group.

This is a work of fiction. Names, characters, places, and incidents either are the product of the author's imagination or are used fictitiously, and any resemblance to actual persons, living or dead, business establishments, events, or locales is entirely coincidental. The publisher does not have any control over and does not assume any responsibility for author or third-party websites or their content.

First edition: January 2008

Library of Congress Cataloging-in-Publication Data

White, Sasha, 1969–
   Wicked / Sasha White.
      p.   cm.
   ISBN-13: 978-0-425-21918-8
   I. Title.
   PS3623.H57885W53 2008
   813'.6—dc22
                                                          2007035996

PRINTED IN THE UNITED STATES OF AMERICA

10   9   8   7   6   5   4   3   2   1

Acknowledgments

There are so many people to thank for their help in getting this story right. First and foremost, J.J. Massa and Beth Williamson, for being there for me through the whole process. In no special order, I'd also like to thank Claudia, Nelson, Jilleena, and Patrick, for talking to me and being so open, and helping me understand so much.

A dedicated life is the life worth living.
You must give with your whole heart.

—Annie Dillard

Prologue

A light scraping across a pierced nipple brought Karl Dawson awake with a pleasurable tingle that went straight to his groin. Nimble fingers flicked the small gold hoop back and forth while another hand smoothed up and down his back. A sigh eased from him, but he didn't open his eyes.

When a third hand took hold of his growing hard-on, he still didn't open his eyes. But he did roll onto his back to give the girls easy access. He'd worked hard to keep them both happy the night before. Letting them get him off, before they all got up, was the perfect way to start the day.

One set of soft lips drifted over his chest and another across his hip bone. As if they'd planned it, one mouth wrapped around a nipple and suckled at the same time wet heat engulfed his cock.

"Wonderful, ladies," he praised softly. "Very nice."

He laid a hand on Marie's back, and his fingers tangled gently in Jan's soft curls. He knew it was Jan sucking his cock without looking. If the way she used her tongue hadn't given it away, the piercing there would've. That meant it was Marie moving between his nipples, teasing him gently.

The three of them had played together before, and he'd trained them to know what he liked—what his body liked. It wasn't their fault he was starting to find their usual sex games boring.

1

"Why is there a woman under your desk?"

Karl Dawson's steps faltered as soon as he entered the office. He stopped walking to enjoy the view of the denim-covered heart-shaped ass sticking out from under his assistant's desk. Definitely female. And it was tilted up at an angle that made his hand itch to spank.

"I've switched sides." The smirk on Graham Nelson's pretty face as he said that made it clear he was full of shit.

Dressed in black slacks, a purple shirt, and a pink tie, he was such a flaming homosexual that Karl often toyed with the urge to hose him down with the fire extinguisher, just to see what would happen.

Instead, all he did was raise an eyebrow, fix his assistant with a look, and deepen his voice slightly. "Graham."

"My friend Lara. She's installing a wireless network for us." Graham stood back from his desk, planted a hand on his out-thrust hip, and eyeballed him. "Your client base has increased thirty percent in the last two months alone. This is needed."

Karl eyeballed him right back. The divorce business *was* booming, and Graham was right—his legal services were in high demand with no signs of slowing down.

Shit. He *hated* changes made to his computer. Computers were not his friend. Anything beyond email gave him a headache and Graham knew it. "If you put more crap on my computer and my life gets more difficult . . . so does yours."

"Actually . . ." A muffled voice came from Graham's desk, and Karl tried not to notice his body's reaction to the delectable ass wiggling and waving as the woman backed out from beneath it.

She stood casually, thick black locks streaming down her back as she tossed her head and met his gaze head-on. "Once I get my hands on your laptop you'll be able to connect to the Internet from pretty much anywhere in the building, including the restaurant downstairs. We've set up a dedicated server for your files and all your data has already been transferred. I can teach you how to navigate the new programs in less than fifteen minutes, and life will be easier for you both."

Graham waved his hand airily. "Trust me on this, Mr. Dawson. The upgrade will make my job easier, therefore your life simpler."

The words barely registered in his mind as Karl watched Lara check him out. He recognized the appreciation in her gaze and an answering hunger stirred inside him.

He arched an eyebrow her way. "You're going to teach me?"

"Sure." Her smile turned suggestive. "I have no problem teaching a man how to do things right."

"I don't usually need instruction from my women."

She shrugged. "All men need instruction at some point or another."

Fire leapt to life inside of him, but Karl didn't bother to respond. It had been a hell of a morning and he wasn't really in the mood to deal with attitude from anyone, sexy or not.

And she was very sexy.

Bright blue eyes, smooth honey colored skin, and lush cock-sucking lips made her very tempting; but she wore her arrogant attitude like a second skin. A second skin that blanketed a small, tight body in faded jeans and a skimpy pink t-shirt that made it clear she wasn't wearing a bra. When his gaze lingered on her pert breasts, her nipples hardened and surprisingly, his mouth watered.

The image of her stretched out on his bed, tied down and still trying to tell him what to do flashed through his mind and he shook his head. She'd be too much work.

"I'll be in my office when you're ready." He strode into his office, aware of her eyes on him as he walked, and closed the door.

Spring fever had hit full force this year and he'd been fighting his restlessness for a while. How it happened he didn't know.

Work was great. The divorce business was booming, and as one of the city's top sharks in that pool, he was making more than enough money to make him happy.

Women had always been easy for him. He wasn't blessed with particularly good looks—his blond hair had just enough curl to make it unruly and his brown eyes were nothing to speak of—but women still wanted him. Even more so since he'd started making the big bucks.

He could get as much sex as he wanted, in any way he wanted, and he'd enjoyed it a lot in the past. But lately, sex just didn't seem to be enough to hold his interest, and the fighting and negotiating of high profit divorce work was becoming tedious.

At least when he was at The Dungeon, he knew it was *him* the women wanted. When the divorcées and society ladies he met through work hit on him, he was sure they wanted the successful lawyer, not the man.

And yet, last night, for the third time in the last two weeks he'd left The Dungeon alone.

The underground sex club had been his playground for many years, and his reputation as a Dominant had grown so much that offers for companionship were never lacking. More than a couple of offers for sexual play had been made the night before, but he'd turned them all down.

If one of his regular playmates, Jan or Marie, had been there he might've been into it. His girls were always eager to please, and that was always fun, but he hadn't been in the mood for someone new. Strange considering he used to thrive on the challenge of training a new submissive, or just having a new girl for one night. But the usual sex games had become . . . boring.

Hell, his life had become boring. Something was missing.

A sharp rap on his door had him shaking his thoughts off and focusing on the day ahead. "Come on in."

Lara strode into his office, a challenging smile on her lips and a gleam in her eye. "Ready for your lessons?"

This one was definitely not boring.

Yet, something tightened in Karl's chest when he looked at her, and he wasn't sure if it was annoyance, amusement, or . . . arousal.

Lara Fox couldn't help herself, she loved flirting too much.

She'd flirt pretty much anytime, anywhere, and with anyone. It made her feel good—made her feel strong and sexy, and in control.

Normally she didn't initiate flirtations unless she was looking to pick someone up for a night, or hustling him at the pool table. But Graham's boss was pretty yummy, and she was suddenly very hungry. Despite his obviously expensive suit, crisp navy blue tie and polished shoes, Karl Dawson had an edge to him.

Maybe it was the scar running through his eyebrow, or the hint of ink she saw on his neck when he turned his head and his hair shifted. Then again, it could just be the look in his dark-chocolate-colored eyes—the look of a man who knew his way around a woman's body.

"I promise I won't hurt you," she said when he didn't reply to her taunt about the lessons. "Just show me your laptop and we can get started."

"Sweetheart, you couldn't hurt me if you tried," he said as he opened up his laptop.

Oh, you might be surprised, Lara thought with a hidden smile. But instead of saying so, she winked and played a little more. "Is that an invitation?"

Dark eyes flashing, he held out his hands, palms up, and flashed her a cocky grin. When he didn't say anything further Lara sauntered around the desk to stand beside his chair. Their eyes met and a tingle zinged through her.

So tempting to just straddle his lap and plant a big kiss on him. Just to see his reaction. Well, and to enjoy it too, because there was no doubt in her mind that she'd enjoy kissing him.

A small smile graced her lips and she turned to the laptop, bent at the waist, and started tapping out commands without another word. The silence stretched and the tension built. Lara's blood heated and she shifted her stance, arching her back a bit more and locking her knees as she bent over the desk.

If they'd met at another time in another place, she was sure they'd have a hell of a good time for a few hours. But he was her friend's boss, and that could make things awkward when she wanted to walk away—and she was always the one to walk away—so it wasn't going to happen. Which meant she had to keep her hormones in check.

The heat of him next to her as she worked was distracting.

She worked faster, keeping her eyes on the computer, but she couldn't help flirting with the fire just a little bit by shifting her weight so that her hip brushed against his shoulder, then away again.

Karl's chair shifted back a little and she felt his eyes on the tribal tattoo on the small of her back, her ass, her legs. The desire to be touched, to connect—just for a short time—awakened inside her and she closed her eyes briefly.

This was not good. Not good at all. She needed to get out of there. Her lunch break was almost over and she had her own job to get back to.

Yeah, that was it. Work.

She gave herself a mental head slap and straightened up.

"Okay, look at this," she called him forward. "It's obvious you're familiar with the Internet and email, which means you also know that it's not always reliable. With the dedicated server you can store all your files on here and they can be accessed by anyone with the passwords."

All business, Lara went on to explain what the passwords were, and how he could change them to his own. How he could make certain areas accessible only to him, and leave others open to Graham and anyone else he needed to share information with. She showed him the new programs she'd installed at Graham's request, all the files they'd already transferred, and showed him how to work the system, as well as the advantages of the wireless connection.

"Got it?" she asked.

"You were right," he nodded. "These changes will make things a bit easier. Thank you."

She chuckled. "Try not to choke on the words."

"Hey, it doesn't happen often, so when it does, I don't mind admitting I was wrong."

She perched her butt on the edge of his desk and leaned back on her hands. The posture thrust her breasts forward, and the air sizzled between them as his gaze swept over her. "A little arrogant, aren't you?"

"Not arrogant." He grinned wickedly. "Confident."

Her mouth ran away without her brain again. "It's been my experience that men as *confident* as you are often overcompensating for something. What do you think about that?"

"I think you haven't experienced me."

An unladylike bark of laughter jumped from her lips. "Oh ho! Is that a challenge?"

His eyes darkened and his smile became almost predatory. "Maybe it's a warning."

Lara's heart pumped faster and blood raced through her veins. Suddenly she was feeling very *alive*.

She pushed away from the desk and started for the door. "Too bad. I've always been a sucker for a challenge." Her hand was on the doorknob when his next softly spoken words halted her in her steps.

"But a warning scares you off?"

Now *that* was a challenge.

2

She should've ignored it.

Lara's instincts told her Karl Dawson was trouble, but he was the type of trouble she just could not resist. Even as her gut had told her to forget it, she'd turned back to meet his mocking gaze. Now, six hours later, she was putting on mascara and debating if she wanted to wear panties or not.

The night was going to end with sex, there was no doubt in her mind about that. But it was all she'd let happen. She wasn't shy about her body's needs, and there was no denying the chemistry between them, but it wouldn't last.

It never did.

"I can't believe you're going out with Graham's boss," Peter said from his perch on her bed.

Peter was a full-time writer and Graham's lover. He owned the small house they all lived in. Situated on the now-trendy Commercial Drive near downtown, it was his family's home. He'd inherited it when his parents retired to the island, and it was the perfect location for her because it was a quick drive to work, and the drive had many restaurants and a few pubs popping up.

The two men lived upstairs in the main part of the house while Lara rented the basement apartment and banked every cent she could so that someday soon she'd be able to buy her own house.

It didn't need to be a big one, but she wanted something that was all hers. Something no one could ever take away from her.

"He seemed okay with it," she said with a shrug. Not that it mattered.

Even though her place was technically separate, the guys had made it a point to become friends with her since she'd moved in just over a year ago. Now they acted like roommates, watching movies and eating together occasionally, as well as nosing into each other's lives. Or trying to, anyway.

The guys shared everything with her, sometimes oversharing, but she kept her secrets. They thought they knew her pretty well, but out of necessity Lara had learned to be a good actress at a very young age.

"We're not enough for you, huh?"

She arched an eyebrow and smirked. "Maybe if I ever got more out of you than a kiss and a cuddle, but as it stands—no."

Peter met her gaze in the mirror. "All you need to do is say the word."

She tensed. "And how would Graham feel about that?"

His full lips lifted on one side and a dimple appeared in his stubbled cheek. "He probably wouldn't like it as much as I would."

That was an understatement, and they both knew it. While Peter was openly bisexual, Graham wasn't. He was also in love with Peter.

Every now and then the sexual tension would grow between her and Peter, and Lara knew that if it weren't for Graham they'd have a good time between the sheets. But until Graham was either out of the picture, or invited her into their bed himself, she was staying out of their domestic situation.

"Which is why it's best I find my entertainment elsewhere," Lara said with a wink. "Now fuck off so I can get dressed. I'm meeting him in half an hour and I need some peace before I leave."

Peter left and Lara dressed quickly. She did wear panties under her short flirty skirt, but decided against a bra to go under the black satin camisole she chose to go with it. When she wore a bra, she filled a B-cup perfectly, so one wasn't always necessary, and she liked the touch of the smooth fabric against her bare skin.

After a last once over in the mirror, she grabbed her purse and headed out.

Lara didn't spend a lot of time on her looks. It wasn't because she didn't need to—although thanks to good genetics she really didn't—it was because she knew there was more to her than the way she looked.

Besides that, being pretty wasn't always what it was cracked up to be, it had brought her more grief than happiness. When she was fifteen, a drunken friend of her father's didn't want to take no for an answer. He'd pinned her to the floor and tried to rape her while her father was passed out on the couch. All because she was such a "pretty girl."

She'd cracked his head open with a crystal ashtray, before taking off on her own for good. And she never looked back.

Then she'd learned how to use her looks to her advantage. Men never thought women were good at pool, or darts, or cards, and they certainly didn't concentrate well when the woman flirted and flashed a little cleavage. Her looks had helped her survive on her own, but it was her mind that had taught her how, and when, to use them.

She climbed into her little Honda hatchback and set out for the restaurant Karl had named. The car wasn't fancy, but it was hers, bought and paid for, and she was proud of it. Karl had wanted to pick her up for their date, but she'd nixed that idea fast. She wanted to keep things casual.

From behind the closed blinds of his bedroom window, Peter watched Lara get into her car with mixed feelings. Why he was even paying attention he wasn't sure. It's not like she never went out, or like she never brought men home. He knew she did both on a pretty regular basis. But he'd sensed something while she was getting ready, something new.

She was excited about Graham's boss.

"I'm home." Graham's call from the kitchen was clear. "And I brought sushi for dinner."

Peter scrubbed a hand through his hair and headed for the kitchen. "Great, I'm starved."

"I passed Lara just up the road," Graham said as he unpacked the food. "She's meeting my boss for dinner. How weird is that?"

"Not so weird. Most men want Lara when they see her."

"I don't."

He pulled a couple of plates from the cupboard and carried them to the table. "If she was willing to wear a strap-on you wouldn't hesitate to bend over for her."

"Petie!"

Peter turned to smile at his lover. "What? It's true and you know it."

Graham sidled up close to him, putting a hand on his back and stroking it up and down. "I'm with you, I don't need anyone else to make me happy."

Peter knew that was supposed to make him feel good, but it didn't. He loved Graham, but he also loved the feel of a woman every now and then. "What if I need someone else every now and then to satisfy me?"

Graham froze, and then pulled his hand away slowly. "You're not happy with me?"

"No, baby. I am happy with you!" Peter's gut clenched at look on Graham's face. "I love you."

Graham folded his arms across his chest, color creeping over his cheeks as he cocked a hip. "Then what exactly are you trying to say?"

"You know I'm bi—you've always known. Sometimes I just crave the feel of a woman beneath me. I admit I've thought of inviting Lara to join us sometime."

Graham's brow furrowed and his bottom lip thrust out. "I thought you gave women up."

"I don't know that I'll ever give them up completely." He reached out and cupped a hand at the back of Graham's neck and pulled him close for a kiss. "But I'll always want you."

It didn't take her long to find the right place. The little Italian restaurant was buried between a print shop and a new age retail store, and she was even on time.

"Not what I was expecting," she said as joined her dinner partner.

He was eye-catching, even dressed to blend with the crowd in dark slacks and a button-up shirt. Her eyes had gone straight to him at the small table along the far wall the minute she'd stepped through the door. Maybe it was the curls. The dark blond looked soft and enticing. The urge to reach out and touch was strong.

He gave a small smile when she was settled in her seat. "You don't like it?"

"I didn't say that." She looked around the place—red and white checked tablecloths, candles in each centerpiece, and the dark-skinned couple at the kitchen doorway arguing passionately made the atmosphere homey, yet still intimate. "It's just not what I expected."

"I'm going to take that as a compliment," he said with a rough chuckle.

Lara met his laughing brown eyes and grinned, relaxing a little. "It was meant as one. Predictability is boring."

Karl was intrigued. "Do you think it's really as simple as that? Keep things unpredictable and life won't be boring?"

"Why not?" Lara leaned back in her chair, her smile bright and flirtatious. "Life is meant to be lived. That means experiencing new things all the time and not getting stuck in a rut."

"You've never been in a rut?"

Something dark flickered in her eyes, and then it was gone. "Not me. I'll try anything once and do the good stuff again . . . and again." She leaned forward, putting her arms on the table and plumping up her cleavage nicely. "What about you?"

Karl's blood heated when he heard her say the magic words. "You'll do anything once? That's a pretty bold statement."

"I'm a pretty bold girl."

"Yes, you are, aren't you?" So very different from what he'd always wanted in a woman—in a submissive. As much as it surprised him, there was no denying his body's reaction to her; and *that*, he wanted to explore. "But I've met many who say that—not everyone can back it up."

She laughed outright. "Oh, I can back it up. When I want to."

His balls tightened and he smiled. This was going to be interesting.

A small movement behind her showed the waitress on her way over so he changed the subject. "Would you like some wine with dinner?"

She shook her head. "I don't need alcohol to have a good time."

Even more intriguing. He waited for the waitress to leave to get their drinks before leaning forward and gazing at her intently. "What *do* you need to have a good time?"

"Nothing but a willing partner." She winked playfully. "And sometimes I don't even need that."

He laughed. She was a spitfire, and he was officially interested.

Their drinks arrived and they ordered their meals. He watched Lara as she looked around the restaurant, sipped her iced tea, and flirted with him. She wasn't being shy about it at all. She went from sassy and bold, to sweet and almost little girlish at times, making his pulse pick up when she looked at him from under her lashes, and nibbled on the luscious bottom lip that had him imagining lots of long, wet, and sloppy blowjobs.

Oh yeah, he wanted her on her knees before him, smiling prettily and begging for his cock. "You'll try anything once, huh?"

She shrugged. "Pretty much, yeah."

"Pretty much? Or you will?"

It was an outright challenge, and he waited expectantly to see if she was really as bold and adventurous as she claimed. If she just might have a submissive streak, a need to please.

He watched as she leaned forward, her silky top shifting enough to tease him with a quick peek at the deeper pink of a nipple before she shifted and it was gone. His eyes traveled over the smooth skin of her neck to see her lips part slightly and her tongue press sassily against little white teeth as she watched him look her over.

Neither spoke, and the tension built. Hot, electric, and . . . exciting. That's what he was feeling—excitement. For the first time in too long, he was captivated.

"How is everything with your meal?"

Just like that, and the moment was broken, and surprisingly, Karl wasn't sure how he felt about it.

"Lara?" he asked.

She broke their gaze and smiled up at the waitress. "It's wonderful, thank you."

The waitress left and they went back to eating. After she swallowed another forkful of penne she gave him a soft smile. "So Karl, what happened to turn a tattooed tough guy into a lawyer?"

Surprise rippled through him. There was no way to completely hide the tribal tat that crept up his neck, even when in a suit and tie, but it was rare for someone to come right out and comment on it. "I decided the best revenge on those who said I'd never amount to anything more than a street thug was to prove them wrong."

She looked like she wanted to ask more, but she let it go with a smile, and his opinion of her went up another notch. Sexy *and* smart.

Now he really wanted to see if she'd do anything once, and exactly what she'd do again, and again.

3

Lara squeezed her thighs together under the table as the waitress cleared their plates and asked if they wanted any dessert. She shook her head and Karl sent the pretty waitress away with a smile.

The meal had been great, and the company much more interesting than she'd anticipated.

Normally when she spent too much time with a guy, some of the attraction wore off. They'd prattle on about sports and cars and how great they really were, and she'd just try to imagine how big their cock was. It wasn't absolutely necessary for a guy to have a big cock to satisfy her in bed, but it sure helped pass the time to wonder if he did.

Plus, she'd learned that most men who went on and on about themselves, or their jobs, over dinner were often equally selfish in bed and only size and some stamina could redeem them.

Then there was the opposite.

The men who tried so hard to be romantic, and sweet, and told her how beautiful she was and asked all sorts of questions she'd have to dodge. They'd be giving in bed, often going down on her and trying to make sure she came before they did. But sometimes that was almost worse because it felt like they were trying to make love, when all she wanted was to fuck.

Love was a trap Lara refused to think about.

She watched Karl's sure movements as he pulled out his wallet and laid some cash on the table. He was certainly confident, and the throbbing between her thighs hinted that he had reason to be.

They were both quiet as they stood to leave, and it was a nice quiet. Not comfortable exactly, there was too much heat bouncing back and forth between them for it to be entirely comfortable, but it was nice.

As soon as they stepped outside the restaurant his hand settled at the small of her back and heat seeped into her bloodstream. Oh yeah, this was going to be good. Sex with Karl was going to be well worth the effort of actually getting to know him a bit. She'd even enjoyed it, but now she really was ready for dessert.

"This is mine," she said as they neared her little Honda. When they were between the cars she turned and put her hand on his chest. "Dinner was nice. Thank you."

"You're welcome."

She gazed into his heavy-lidded eyes and waited . . . and waited . . . and finally, unable to wait any longer, went up on her tiptoes and kissed him.

His muscles flexed beneath the palm of her hand and his lips parted, letting her control the kiss for a brief moment before his hand cupped the back of her neck and he took over. His body pressed against hers and she fell back against her car, enjoying the pressure of his hardness against her as his tongue thrust into her mouth and wiped all thought from her mind.

Hot breath filled her as their tongues rubbed and thrust and danced together. Her breasts swelled and ached, her legs spreading as she undulated against him. Then his fingers wrapped in her hair and tightened. She couldn't move her head and Karl took full advantage, nipping at her bottom lip sharply before pulling back.

She gasped for breath, the sting in her lip making her pussy clench. "I'm ready for dessert now. How about you?" she asked breathlessly.

He stepped back, his hands falling to his side as shutters came down over the heat in his eyes. "I think that was enough for now. The perfect end to the evening."

What?

He leaned forward, pressed a quick hard kiss to her still parted lips, and then walked away without another word.

"Hey!" she called after him. "What was that?"

He stopped and turned around, an amazingly cocky smirk on his lips. "When you're ready to promise to truly do anything once, give me a call."

Stunned, Lara watched him leave, and bit back a few choice words. Part of her really wanted to let him have it . . . but another part of her refused to let him know just how disappointed she was.

He might've turned her down, Lara thought as she pulled open her car door and slid into the driver's seat, but she'd never chased a man in her life. And she wasn't going to start now.

4

Karl watched the blonde's sultry hip swing as she walked away, and once again wondered what the fuck his problem was. Her offer to do anything for him was for real, but unlike Lara's questionable claim of a similar attribute the other night, it hadn't stirred the least bit of interest.

In fact, the only thing that had raised any interest in him lately had been Lara. Strange, considering he normally liked sweet and submissive—not sassy and bold—but there it was.

Being a Dominant had come naturally to him. In fact, he'd never even realized that he was controlling and directing women in the bedroom until one of his lovers, a submissive, had explained it to him. He'd been in his early twenties when that had happened, and she'd introduced him to The Dungeon, and the lifestyle that had helped him find his true nature.

More than ten years in the lifestyle, and he'd become accustomed to women as adept and comfortable in it as he was.

Maybe that was the problem.

Lara had tempted him, but at the end of the night he'd still walked away. Something told him that if he got involved with her, it wouldn't be simple.

Then again, maybe it was time for things to stop being so simple.

He glanced over at a couple of other regulars he knew. He'd watched them scene before, and the submissive was a bit of a brat, the Dom having to discipline her often. It was obviously a dynamic that worked for them, but he'd never been into the strict discipline aspect of D/s.

He considered himself a loving Dom, one who could be firm when needed, but who, above all, rewarded submission with praise, affection, and pleasure.

"Another one incoming, Master Karl," Marc the bartender warned as he set another beer in front of him.

Karl felt the presence of a warm body at his right side and turned his head. "Hello, Marie, how are you tonight?"

"Eager and willing, Sir." The redhead's smile was sincere and the spark in her eyes attractive.

Sweet, eager, and submissive. Exactly what he'd always enjoyed.

Yet, he still wasn't interested. Despite that, he put his arm around her and cupped her rear fondly. "That's nice to hear, sweetie. But I'm not up for any games tonight. You girls about wore me out last weekend so I'm gonna take a pass this time. You go have some fun without me."

Her bottom lip quivered and he shook his head sharply once. He didn't want to see her pout.

"What the hell am I even doing here?" he muttered after she'd disappeared back into the crowded club.

"No idea, sir."

Karl met Marc's gaze and chuckled wryly. "Aren't bartenders supposed to have all the answers?"

"Some things people need to figure out for themselves," Marc replied with a grin.

"And I'm not going to do it sitting here at this bar, am I?" Karl tossed a bill next to his still half-full beer, and headed for the door.

He weaved through the crowd, not even bothering to look at the people around him. He climbed the stairs and sucked in a deep breath of fresh air when he hit the street. It had rained again. The pavement was wet and the air was fresh and clean.

Spring had arrived. Spring was a good time for a change. Maybe waiting for Lara to call him this past week had been the wrong tactic.

Normally he'd be a hundred percent confident she'd call. Women always called—but she *was* different. It was what had intrigued him. A week later and he was still intrigued.

Now he just had to figure out how to proceed. It would be different with Lara. She wasn't someone in the BDSM scene, and she wasn't someone in the society scene. And he was already pretty sure she was someone he'd want more than one night with.

Pulling the keys for his truck from his pocket he wished they were the keys for his bike. A nice long drive through the mountains with the wind against his face would be welcome right about then.

Laughter and catcalls from the pub across from The Dungeon caught his attention as he crossed the street and started for the black Dodge Ram he'd parked half a block down. His steps slowed for a minute as he looked in the windows of the pub. The live band and boisterous crowd was easily heard from where he stood.

It sounded alive and enthusiastic, just like Katie Long had been that night almost a year earlier when they'd had drinks there.

Katie's enthusiasm for life and unique blend of innocence and open sexuality had hooked him pretty good. She'd been a wonderful change from the jaded and angry women he met through work, and the overeager and overexperienced women he had as playmates. She'd been the change that had given birth to this strange restlessness, and now, another eager, but obviously experienced, woman kept sashaying through his mind.

One that was loud, and bold, and enthusiastic . . . and who was shaking her ass on the dance floor of the very same pub.

Tucking his keys back into his pocket he headed for the pub's entrance. It was time to see if she really would try anything once, and do the good things again and again.

5

The band was playing and the heavy beat matched the low level throb in Lara's blood as she moved. The heat of admiring eyes drifted over her skin. There were so many, male and female, all hot with passion that fired her blood.

She'd take one of them home that night. A man. A man with a big cock, plenty of passion, and lots of stamina to help chase away the hot dreams of that arrogant egotistical . . . lawyer.

Large hands rested on her hips and a body brushed against her back. She glanced over her shoulder and winked at the bald college boy who'd moved in to dance with her.

She shouldn't call him a *boy*, he was probably only younger than her by a year or two, but he wasn't man enough to inspire a stronger title. His excitement and eagerness fairly bled from him as he rubbed his groin against her ass in an effort to be sexy. It might be a little mean of her to tease him, but she couldn't stop herself.

She bent forward at the waist, pressing her hips back against him, and did a bump and grind that had her own body softening, readying itself for action. With a flip of her head, she straightened up, back arched as she rested her head against his shoulder and undulated against him in time with the music.

"You are so fucking hot," he panted in her ear, his hands slipping over the smooth flesh of her belly that was bared by her crop top.

She spun in his arms just as the last notes of the song were struck, and the music faded into the crowd's applause.

The band said they were going to take a short break, and everyone started to drift off the dance floor. It was time to rehydrate.

"Thanks for the dance," she said to the boy, and spun on her heel to leave.

He grabbed her arm, halting her steps. "That's it? Come on, baby. Let's find a dark corner and get to know each other better."

She looked at his hand on her arm before raising her gaze to his. She gave him a look that any smart man would recognize as a warning. College boy wasn't stupid, and he released his grip.

"Yeah," he said with a sneer. "Whatever."

Lara headed for the bar without another word and immediately spotted the lean blond parked there in leather pants and a snug black t-shirt.

Oh shit.

Her heart kicked in her chest and every hair on her body stood on end. Karl looked so fucking good her mouth actually started to water. Saliva pooled on her tongue and her pussy clenched in recognition of what it hungered for. She'd been able to resist the lure of his challenge when she only had images of him in a suit and tie in her mind, but this . . . she had no resistance to the living fantasy in front of her.

Even worse, she wasn't sure she wanted to.

Altering her course slightly she headed straight for him. "Well hello there, sexy. How are you tonight?"

"Feeling pretty good after watching your little show there," he replied. "You move very well, sweetie."

Pleasure swept over her at his compliment and she gave herself a mental kick in the ass. She knew she moved well, she didn't need him to tell her that. Plus, he'd called her *sweetie*.

Lara eyed him. She realized he was being sincere, and that sent a wave of pure desire rushing through her veins. Normally she hated it when men called her sweetie or baby or darlin', or any number of chauvinistic endearments. But Karl's lazily spoken words were different somehow.

"Thanks," she said before smiling at the bartender and asking for a bottle of water.

When he set the water on the bar, Karl handed him a bill before she could, and the bartender walked away.

"Thank you, again." She turned to face Karl, stepping closer so that her hip brushed against his leather-clad knee.

She let her eyes roam over him, not bothering to hide the need simmering in her blood. Why should she? She'd made it pretty clear the other night that she wanted him. He'd been the one to walk away.

Remembering that, she shifted, a little unsure exactly how to handle him now. Unsure of how she *wanted* to handle him now.

As if he could read her thoughts, Karl's lips tilted slightly and the lines around his eyes crinkled, making the small scar that ran through his left eyebrow shift. "You didn't call," he said.

Not wanting to shout in the loud bar or let him sense her momentary doubts, she shifted closer. When she moved, he spread his knees wider and she automatically filled the spot.

"Why didn't you call?" he repeated.

She arched a brow at him. "Why didn't *you* call?"

He chuckled. "Because you're the one who needs to decide if you're really willing to do anything at least once."

Would she? Wicked heat zinged from her brain to her sex in answer and she grinned. Payback could be so much fun, sometimes.

"Follow me?" she challenged.

His chocolate eyes darkened and his lips twitched as he stood so they were chest to chest. "Lead the way."

With a little extra swing in her hip, she headed for the back of the pub.

The band was starting up again and they were going against the stream of people heading back to the dance floor. Karl's hand rested on the curve of her hip, the heat of his body close behind her as they passed the men's room, then the ladies' room, and went straight out the back door.

She'd been antsy and horny before she saw him, but in the past three minutes her body had started to burn from the inside out. Everything in her was centered on having him—he was not going to walk away from her again. She was in control this time.

Karl was all man—all very sexy, very primal man. She might not know exactly what was going on between them, but she did know one thing for sure—she was woman enough to take him on, and revel in it.

The cool night air hit her skin and a shiver ripped through her. She glanced around the empty parking lot, no real plan in her mind, just animalistic need driving her to do what came naturally. She started to head for her car, but then spotted the narrow walkway between the pub and the darkened building next to it. A big leafy tree almost hid the small space.

It was perfect.

Without a word she entered the small passage and went about ten steps before stopping. She turned and faced Karl, who was looking at her with a mix of curiosity and approval.

"You," she said, putting her hands on his chest and gently shoving him against the cement wall of the pub. "Are not walking away from me this time."

She leaned in, pressing her body against his fully, and ran her tongue over the tattoo on his neck. His pulse jumped as she nibbled her way toward his ear only to have her head pulled back sharply. The hand that was suddenly wrapped in her hair tightened, and her pussy throbbed in answer.

"Oooh," she cooed in appreciation, but the sound was cut off when his head came down and his mouth covered hers.

Lara struggled to remember her plan as Karl's flavor washed over her. He tasted so damn good—hot, potent, and male. His muscles flexed and danced under her hand as she swept them down over his chest and flat abs to his belt. Her fingers shook with her eagerness as she unsnapped and unzipped his pants.

Pushing aside the supple leather, she groaned into Karl's mouth when his cock leapt into the palm of her hand.

Oh yeah! He was well built all over.

The grip on her hair tightened and her head was tugged back. Karl's mouth slid over her cheek to her ear, where he nipped at the sensitive lobe, sending bolts of pleasure straight to her pussy. "What are you gonna do with that, naughty girl?"

She pulled back slightly, shaking her head and dislodging his grip. "I'm going to make it mine," she said as she bent her knees.

Karl watched as Lara knelt in front of him, the moonlight streaming through the tree's leaves and gleaming on the top of her head as her hot breath drifted over his naked cock. She'd surprised him again, in a very good way.

A long lick up the underside of his cock had him sucking in a sharp breath and reaching deep for his self-control as she swirled her tongue over the sensitive head. His balls tightened and he closed his eyes, letting his head fall back against the wall.

His fingers tangled in her soft hair, but he just enjoyed the feel of the silky strands. This was her thing, and he was going to let her do it the way she wanted.

For now.

It felt good, better than good, as she expertly circled the base of his shaft with her fingers and stroked. She caressed the full length of his shaft while her lips were wrapped around the top, gently sucking on the head. She popped him out of her mouth, licking him like a lollipop for a brief moment before taking him deep.

A groan of pleasure rumbled through him, and he let it escape. "Deeper, sugar. Take me as deep as you can," he coached.

He didn't press into her though, he wanted to let her play, let her taste him and get used to the size and feel of him.

He also wanted to see how well she listened.

Another groan eased from his throat when she did as he asked, her hands gripping his thighs as she stretched her jaw and sank down on his cock.

She couldn't take him all, he hadn't expected her to, but she took him deep enough that he was touching the back of her throat. He looked down at her, one hand going to gently cup under her jaw. Karl could feel himself there as she pulled back, then took him deep again.

"Good girl," he murmured when her throat spasmed around him and she pulled back sharply, leaving his cock bobbing in the cool air. "Do it again. I like it when I feel the back of your throat."

She looked up at him, her eyes gleaming in the darkness as she licked her shiny lips. His heart pounded as he waited for her to speak, but she didn't. Instead, one hand wrapped around his shaft again, and she closed her eyes, taking him into her mouth once more. This time, there was no struggle to take him deep.

Her hand stroked in time with her mouth as she sucked, her head going up and down, her speed increasing. Her other hand reached between his legs, wiggling in under the leather low on his hips and cupping his balls. He watched her, just as much pleasure coming from the sight of her at his feet as from the actual sensation of her mouth on him.

He kept his hand beneath her chin where he could feel her pulse pounding, and his cock sliding along her tongue. The sound of her panting breath was music to his ears and his cock swelled. She was working so hard, such a good girl. Such a sassy, sexy, horny, adventurous girl.

Karl's breath caught as his hips thrust forward, everything inside him centering on his cock as pleasure exploded and he gave her all he had.

"Yes, my girl," he cried as she swallowed. "Take it all."

Tremors rippled through him as she continued to suckle him, gently cleaning him before she stood slowly. When she was at her full height she reached up, cupped the back of his head and pulled him down for a kiss. He tasted himself on her tongue as it swept between his lips and into his mouth in one fierce move. Then she was done.

She stepped back, a fingertip wiping the corner of her smiling lips. "I *will* do anything once," she purred before spinning on her heel and walking away.

"Call me," she shouted over her shoulder before she disappeared around the corner of the building.

A laugh bubbled up inside of him and he let it roll out. She was certainly a handful. A very pleasurable, and deliciously wicked, handful.

6

After fighting his inability to concentrate all day, Karl put his laptop in his briefcase and left the office early.

"Go home early, Graham. We'll work on the Zebrowski papers first thing in the morning," he said as he headed for the door.

Karl was already halfway down the stairs when the door swung shut, cutting off Graham's exaggerated whoop of pleasure. He didn't know exactly where he was going, but he needed to get out of that office. He needed to breath, to think . . . to relax.

He stowed his briefcase behind the truck seat, climbed in . . . and sat behind the wheel. He loved his house. It was his private haven, his comfort zone, but it wasn't where he wanted to be right then either.

With a twist of his wrist the truck was alive and he aimed it north. He needed a different kind of comfort.

After almost thirty minutes of fighting traffic, Karl stopped at the entrance to his friend's office and leaned against the doorjamb. The office wasn't huge, but it was big enough and nice enough to impress with a sofa along one wall, the other wall almost all window so anyone in the office could watch the goings on in the nightclub below, and a monster wooden desk.

Behind that monster wooden desk sat Valentine Ward, with a lap full of soft female.

Instead of speaking up and interrupting, Karl watched as his friend ran his hands under the plump blonde's shirt and pulled her closer. Samair Jones moaned and Karl's dick jumped. The sounds a woman made when being touched just right always went straight to his groin.

"Do you guys ever stop?" he asked before he got too turned on.

Val pulled back and peeked around his girlfriend's shoulder. "Not often, but if you're going to stick around I guess we can take a break."

"What? You wouldn't invite me to join in?"

"You passed on that once, and one chance is all you'll ever get."

"Be nice." Samair smacked Val's shoulder and climbed off his lap to stand by his side. "Hey, Karl, how are you doing?"

Warmth filled his chest as he noted how Samair kept her hand on Val's shoulder, as if she couldn't stand to be so near him and not touch.

A few months earlier Val had been set on fulfilling all of Samair's sexual fantasies, including a threesome with two men. The two men had shared women in the past, but Karl, recognizing that his friend was falling in love, had turned down the invitation to be the second when it came to Samair.

Friendships like theirs could withstand a lot, but Karl hadn't been ready to risk it.

"I'm doing pretty good." He walked into the office and dropped onto the sofa along the far wall.

The lights in the nightclub came on, illuminating the window on the other wall, and Credence Clearwater drifted over the speakers. "Kelsey's here," Karl said in explanation.

Kelsey was the head bartender at Risqué. She'd shown up for her shift just as Karl had pulled out his phone to dial Val to let him in.

"Oh! I need to talk to her before the club opens," Samair said. She leaned down and gave Val a slow lazy kiss before heading for the door. "Maybe I'll see you later, Karl?"

"Maybe." He nodded.

Both men watched her leave, and Karl stretched his legs out in front of him, trying to get comfortable. "So, how's married life?"

"We're not married," Val replied.

"May as well be."

Karl felt his friend's gaze on him and he stood. He walked to the window and looked down on the empty club. The lights were on, the music was on, but the club was empty. Sometimes he felt like that.

Giving his head a shake he kept his back to Val. "Not that marriage would be a bad thing for you two. I think you've caught yourself a good woman, buddy."

"There are a few of them out there, y'know."

Normally he would just shrug off Val's comment. They both knew he wasn't a true believer when it came to love and happy endings.

There had been a time when he was. He'd been a hell-raiser from the time he could walk, but his parents had always loved him, believed in him, and each other. Even when aunts and uncles, teachers and counselors, had all told them he was going to end up in jail or dead by the time he was twenty.

He'd been serving a year in juvenile detention for stealing a car when they'd decided to go on a second honeymoon—and their plane had crashed and burned minutes after taking off.

Realizing how much he'd taken for granted, when he turned eighteen and was released, to honor his parents and the faith they'd always had, he'd straightened up and worked to make something of his life. But somehow, after that, no matter how hard he looked, he couldn't see love anywhere. What he had seen were too many marriages turn very ugly very quickly. But this time, he didn't want to shrug off the comment, or his thoughts.

He turned from the window and met Val's gaze. "Did you know when you met Samair that she was a good one? I mean, I remember you wanted her the minute she walked in the club that first night, but it was just lust, right?"

They'd been friends a long time, but the men rarely talked feelings. They didn't need to.

But now, he needed to.

Something in him had shifted, and he was feeling like he'd been caught flat-footed.

"It was more than lust." Val steepled his fingers under his chin and stared at Karl. "It was curiosity, attraction, desire. I was . . . *drawn* to her."

"You fucked her on the desk that night because you were curious?"

"No. I did that because she asked me to, and by the time I was zipping my pants, I was hooked. I just hadn't known it then."

That was a scary thought. "She's totally different from Vera."

Vera was Val's ex-wife, and a true-blue rich snotty bitch. Completely mercenary in going after what she wanted, like most women Karl knew.

"You're right, Samair's nothing like Vera was."

"But she's a lot like the women you used to date before Vera?"

"Karl, what's going on?" Val stood and walked over to him. "One of your subs giving you a hard time?"

"Nah, it's nothing." He gave his head a shake. "Just feeling a little restless, wondering if a change might be a good thing."

"Change can be good." Val took the hint and shifted the subject. "Samair and I like to change things up all the time."

Karl laughed, ignoring the slight twinge of jealousy he felt at his friend's happiness. Val had fought for his happiness, and he deserved it. "Yeah? Does that mean you're going to be my guests at The Dungeon again sometime soon? And maybe play a little this time?"

"I don't think so. We like to keep our games private."

"Yeah, right! Don't try to tell me you two haven't had gone at it in every room of this club."

"Okay, I won't try to tell you that." He clapped a hand on Karl's shoulder. "Let's go shoot some pool before the bar opens. I need to take some of your money."

"Good luck with that, my friend," he laughed as they left the room, feeling good.

7

Three days and he didn't call.

Lara didn't know why she was surprised. Really, he was a man. She'd sucked his cock, he'd gotten off, and she'd probably never see him again.

There were times when that wouldn't bother her, times when the thrill of just doing what she wanted, where and when she wanted, was enough to make her feel perfectly alive. But this wasn't one of those times.

She'd seen the promise of more in Karl's eyes, even though he'd never voiced it, and she'd wanted it.

"Hi, Lara, how are you today?"

Closing the door on any thoughts of Karl, Lara smiled at the guy behind the auto shop counter. "Hey, sexy," she blew a kiss at him. "The only thing that would make my world any better would be a date with you."

"You'd never be able to keep up with me, little girl." The white-haired mechanic said with a laugh and reached out for the case of oil filters she carried.

"That's true, you did wear out—what? Three wives in twenty years?"

"Yes, ma'am." His bony chest puffed up with pride and Lara grinned. "And they're all going to be waiting for me on the other side, so I need to save my strength."

Lara reached for the invoice he'd signed and tore off his copy. "Then I guess it's best we just remain friends isn't it, Jack?"

Before Jack could answer, his grandson came into the room from the garage, wiping his hands on a dirty rag. "When are you gonna stop teasing the old man and go out with me, Lara?"

"Sorry, Ben, I don't date men I have to work with."

"You don't work with me, you deliver auto parts to our shop. There's no conflict there."

"Yeah, but I'd still have to see you the next day, or the day after that . . . and that's not always a good thing." She tucked the invoice into her leather binder and started for the door with a wave. "Have a good day, gentlemen."

The sun was shining brightly and she tugged the bill of her cap down over her eyes. It was a beautiful March afternoon, and she was almost done working for the day. She climbed into the cab of the little Toyota truck with JAY'S AUTO SUPPLIES stenciled along both sides before double-checking the last invoice in her binder.

One more delivery and then she could clock out for the day. Yee haw!

Looking both ways she pulled onto Broadway and headed toward Granville Street. It was almost three o'clock and traffic was starting to get a little nuts, but it didn't bother her. Her patience on the road was what made her so good at her job as an auto parts delivery person. That's not to say she didn't get frustrated at times, but she always remembered she was in a company truck, and managed to keep from flipping anyone off.

Lara liked her job; she got to meet tons of people, but didn't have to worry about any of them getting to nosy or too close. It also gave her freedom to roam the city, and because she'd been at it for a little more than three years, when most drivers were students that didn't last, a certain amount of security.

Security was important to Lara. More important than the not-so-great paycheck she got every two weeks.

Intellectually she knew she craved security for the same reason she was adamant about maintaining her independence and not getting too close to people.

Her childhood had sucked.

Her mother had taken off when she was a toddler, and her alcoholic father had gone from job to job, *when* he sobered up enough to work. She'd learned early on how to take care of herself and by the time she was ten she was hustling pool to buy groceries.

She still hustled pool at least once a week to make extra money on the side, often making two or three times as much at the tables as she did on her paychecks. Her twenty-eighth birthday was coming up soon, and she was determined to own her own home by the time she hit thirty. And she wasn't going to do it by delivering auto parts alone.

She finally made it over the bridge and pulled into the parking lot for her final drop off. As she strode into the garage, the cell phone on her hip started to vibrate and ring. Not recognizing the number on caller ID, she ignored the phone, smiled at the plump counter girl and handed over the spark plugs.

Signed invoice in hand, she pulled the still-ringing phone off her hip as she headed back to the truck. "Hello?"

"You're such a bad girl!" a frantic voice hissed.

"Graham?"

When his voice came back it was pleasant and professional. "Hi, Lara. Yes, it's Graham here. I have a question for you."

"What's going on? You sound weird." She shut the door of the truck behind her and just sat in the driver's seat for a minute.

"Mr. Dawson would like your phone number and I told him I couldn't give it to him without your permission."

Lara heard a rumbling growl in the background and laughed. She could just imagine Karl's impatience with Graham's fussiness.

"So?" Graham prodded. "Would you prefer I tell Mr. Dawson your number, or tell him you're not interested?"

"Put him on the phone, Graham."

There were some muffled words and then Karl's smooth voice was echoing in her ear. "You're a hard woman to get ahold of."

Satisfaction settled heavy in her belly. "I'm a woman who likes things . . . hard."

"And I'm glad for that." A low chuckle rumbled through the phone lines. "In fact, I'd like to explore that fondness of yours a bit more. Will you have dinner with me tonight?"

"Drinks." Dinner had been nice, but she didn't want him thinking they were dating. This was all about satisfying animal urges.

A slight pause then, "You have somewhere specific in mind?"

Thinking quick she named a pub downtown, not far from where she lived. They decided on a time and she hung up with a grin, anticipation already making her sex warm.

Karl ignored the glare Graham was shooting him and put the phone back in the cradle on his assistant's desk. "She's a big girl, Graham. She knows what she's getting into," he said before walking back to his office. *At least she will after tonight.*

He couldn't believe he'd had to actually *order* Graham to call Lara while he was standing there! The man had refused to give him her number when he'd asked, or her email address. It would be touching if it weren't slightly insulting.

On the other hand, knowing that Lara'd kept their encounters to herself pleased him. He liked his private life to be private, and any concerns he'd had about dating a friend of his employee were now gone.

Sasha White

Dating.

It had been a long time since he'd dated someone outside the lifestyle. Hell, it'd been a long time since he'd dated at all. He preferred to keep his life orderly, and that meant work was work, and play was private. Even his play life was kept orderly. Marie and Jan were his usual playmates, and they knew the score. When they were together, they had all of his attention, but when they weren't together, there were no claims on anyone.

Everyone was happy with the casual relationship.

He no longer looked for love in his relationships. He wasn't even sure he believed in love, anymore; not when he made a very good living off the fact that it never lasted. But spending time with Samair and Val had rekindled some spark inside him.

Lara wasn't looking for love either. She was sexy, adventurous, bold, and definitely wild. He'd walked away from her that first night because she wasn't what he was used to. But now he realized that, for him, that just might be the best thing she had going for her.

I can't believe you're going out with him again. I can't believe you haven't kept me up-to-date! I thought that dinner was a one time thing?"

Lara looked past Graham, who was pacing alongside her bed, and met Peter's gaze. The minute Graham had arrived home from work, he'd grabbed Peter and come down to her place, intent on finding out everything that was going on between her and Karl.

"It's not that big of a deal, Graham. Relax." Once again, she had company while she was getting ready for her date, and this time she was going to use it to her advantage.

Ignoring Graham she turned to Peter with a skirt in each hand. "Denim or cotton?"

"You do realize he's a biker, right?" This from the agitated Graham.

"Denim it is," she said as she hung the cotton skirt back up. "And definitely the leather vest."

"Did you hear me?"

"I heard you, Graham. In case you didn't get the hint, I'm ignoring you." If he didn't shut up soon she was gonna tell him to fuck off, and *not* in a playful way.

This was why she didn't have friends. When people got too close they always tried to tell her what to do, or how to live her life.

Graham stopped and stared at her.

She met his gaze head-on and shrugged out of her robe. Standing there in nothing but a black lace thong, she glared at him and snapped. "What?"

His brow puckered and he looked at her with hurt puppy dog eyes. "I just don't want you to get hurt, sweetie."

"I'm not going to get hurt, Graham. I'm just going to get laid." She stepped into the short denim skirt and pulled it up.

"Mr. Dawson is a good boss, and I like my job." Graham was working himself into a real tizzy. "But the man is supercynical when it comes to women. They throw themselves at him all the time and he just acts as if it's his due. He really is hot, Lara, and I can see why you'd want to go out with him—I've even had a fantasy or two about him myself, but that's not the point—"

"Then get to the point," Lara interrupted as she did up the snaps on her custom leather vest.

He heaved a sigh. "In the three years I've been working for him, never once has he mentioned a girlfriend. He doesn't date women, he just uses them."

"First off, just because he doesn't mention a girlfriend to you doesn't mean he doesn't have one, or ten. Secondly, *I don't care.* I'm not looking for a boyfriend. I'm only planning on using him for a night myself, so we should get along just fine."

"Lara—"

"Peter!"

"Come on, Graham," Peter said as he got up from his position propped up on the pillows of her bed. "Let's go upstairs and I'll let you give me a massage."

"But . . ."

Lara watched as Peter stared at Graham, and Graham's cheeks flushed in response. The tension in the air shifted and even Lara's blood started to heat. There was some silent communication going on there, and it was hot!

"Have a good time," Peter said as he followed Graham out of the bedroom. "And be safe!"

Of course she'd be safe. After all, if she didn't look after herself, who would?

Lara gave herself a once over in the mirror. Her eyes were

lined and smoky looking, her lips coated with a deep crimson that would draw all eyes there, and hopefully remind Karl of just how well she could use her mouth. The leather vest fit perfect. It was tight enough to push her boobs together and give her cleavage, and the skirt was just loose enough to hang suggestively on the curve of her hips.

She looked just how she wanted to look—sassy, sexy, and slightly naughty.

She's going to get hurt, Peter."

Peter heard the concern in Graham's voice, and he reached out for his lover. Brushing his thumb over the palm of Graham's hand, he smiled. "No, she's not. Honestly, Graham, from what you've told me about your boss and what I know about Lara, I'd say he's the one that might get hurt."

"But—"

"But nothing. It's none of our business anyway. If Lara needs someone to talk to, she knows where we are. If your boss hurts her, I know where he lives."

Graham gazed at him with big soft eyes and he felt ten feet tall and bulletproof. "You'd do that? You'd go punch out my biker boss if he hurt Lara?"

"I would. You know I love our prickly housemate just as much as you do."

Something flashed across Graham's face and he pulled back a little. "You love her?"

"Graham," he warned. He really thought they were past the jealous-possessive stage.

"I'm just asking."

He stood and pulled off his t-shirt before reaching for the snap on his jeans. "And I'm waiting for my massage."

Peter watched as Graham took the hint and went down the hall. When he entered the living room with a blanket and the bottle of baby oil, Peter's heart clenched.

His boy looked a little lost.

Naked, he stepped up and took the blanket from Graham. He tossed it on the floor, and pressed his body against his lover's. "I changed my mind. I don't want a massage anymore."

Graham bit his lip and stepped back, looking everywhere but at him. "What do you want?"

Peter opened his heart and put all the love he had in his gaze as he cupped Graham's head and forced him to meet his look head-on. "You."

With that, he stepped closer again and pinned Graham to the wall, his head lowering to show him exactly how much he wanted him.

8

Lara was already at the pool table when Karl entered the pub. He stood and watched her from a distance for a few minutes. She was good, but he could beat her. She played her opponent more than the table. Bending, stretching, and smiling flirtatiously.

Her tight leather vest plumped up her cleavage deliciously, and her short skirt showed off legs that every man in there wanted wrapped around his waist. No, she was no sweet submissive miss—but she was a dirty girl through and through. One who was willing to try anything once.

When she flipped back her hair, bent over, and sent the eight ball into the corner pocket with a sure stroke, he stepped forward with a small smile. "Nice work."

She winked at him as she tucked the bills from the edge of the table into her hip pocket. "Thanks. You wanna play?"

He couldn't hold back the images that flooded his mind at *that* invitation, and he grinned. "Oh yeah, but not pool. Let's grab a seat."

He pointed to a booth near the back corner and they headed toward it. When she slid in one side, he fought his natural urge to slide in next to her, and settled in across the table. The waitress was there immediately, smiling at him and bending over the table to give him a good view down her little tank top. "What can I do for you tonight?"

"Lara?" he asked.

When she ordered a cola, he ordered a beer and sent the waitress away with a lazy smile.

"Do women hit on you everywhere you go?"

He slouched back in his seat and cocked an eyebrow at her. "Do men hit on you everywhere you go?"

Her husky chuckle filled the air between them and a knowing look passed between them. They were a lot alike.

"You don't like to play pool?" she asked.

"I do, but there are other games I'd rather play with you. Ones that will help us get to know each other better."

She leaned forward, her eyes sparkling, her smile wicked. "Do you really want to get to know me better, or do you just want to fuck me?"

What *did* he want from her?

He didn't bother checking out the cleavage displayed so temptingly before him, he knew she was sexy. Instead, he gazed into her eyes. Searching past the spark of desire there, he saw the walls she'd built to protect her thoughts, and he wanted to knock those walls down. He wanted to know what lay beneath the surface.

And he wanted to bend her over and sink his cock in deep.

"Both," he told her. "I think you and I can embark on a journey together—a very pleasurable one."

Tilting her head to the side she narrowed her eyes at him. "Stop talking like a lawyer."

"I'm not talking like a lawyer. I'm talking like a Dom, sugar."

She sat back, surprised. "A Dom? As in, tie me up and spank me?"

He chuckled. "Something like that, yes."

The waitress arrived with their drinks and Lara watched as he paid her, tipping heavily before sending her away with an absent smile.

A Dom.

Damn, that sorta sucked, she'd been looking forward to having that delicious cock of his buried deep inside her. She hadn't had a good hard fuck in way too long, but she wasn't into being spanked.

"I don't know," she said, shaking her head slowly. "I am not a submissive person."

"I think you might surprise yourself. You enjoyed sucking my cock the other night right?"

His small smile was starting to irritate her. "Yeah, but that's not a submissive thing. Men are ruled by their dicks. If I can rule the dick, I can rule the man. That's not exactly a submissive way of thinking, is it?"

"So you got no pleasure from hearing my groans of pleasure, or words of praise? No satisfaction in feeling my cock throb against your tongue as my come filled your mouth?"

His words filled her head, clouding her thoughts as the memory of the other night filled her mind. His hand in her hair, his cock in her mouth, his voice being the only thing she heard beyond the pounding of her own rushing blood as he growled his satisfaction.

She'd swallowed for him. Something she'd never done before. More than that, he was right, she'd enjoyed the whole thing. Walking away from him then had been a point of pride she'd paid for when she was alone in bed with her vibrator.

She'd never shied from a challenge before, yet Karl's words didn't *feel* like just a challenge. They felt like an . . . invitation? She gave herself a mental head slap. Did it really matter? She wanted him, and she *would* try anything once.

So she straightened her spine, thrust out her breasts and boldly met his gaze. "Do I have to call you Master?"

"Master, Sir, Karl." He shrugged. "It doesn't matter. You can call me what you want, whatever feels natural."

Excitement heated her blood and kicked her pulse up a notch. "Okay, how do we do this?"

"Why don't we start with something simple?"

"I'm ready when you are."

His voice lowered. "Are you wearing panties?"

Adrenaline surged through her. "Yeah."

"Take them off, please."

She started to slide out of the booth only to be stopped by his foot blocking her way. She glanced from the black boot to the man across the table, her forehead wrinkling. "Excuse me?"

"Stay here and take them off," he commanded softly. "You proved the other night that you were adventurous when it came to taking risks in public, this should be nothing to you."

He was right—it was nothing. So why was her heart suddenly pounding so hard it vibrated through her chest?

Without bothering to think about it, she shifted forward on her seat a little and reached under the table. Keeping her eyes locked with his, she slid her fingers up her outer thighs and under her denim skirt. She planted her feet on the floor, lifted her hips and tugged at the elastic until the thong slipped from between her cheeks and down her legs.

Bunching the lace in one fist she felt the damp proof of her excitement against the palm of her hand, and pride zipped through her.

"Can I get you anything, sir? Another beer?" The waitress stood at the edge of their table, eyeing Karl.

Deliberately, Lara put her hand on the table between them, and opened it up, offering Karl her panties. Karl smiled his approval and reached for them while he spoke. "No, thank you. I have everything I need for now."

Lara tried not to smirk as the waitress stomped away. When

she saw Karl lift the bundle of lace to his face and inhale, her moment of satisfaction faded into a blur of uncertainty.

"You smell wonderful," he said. "Already turned on, are you?"

"Yeah." She shrugged. Trying not to let him see just how affected she truly was.

"Yes," he said.

"Yes, what?"

"When I ask you a question, I'd like you to answer clearly. Yeah, isn't a proper answer."

"Okay." She nodded, feeling like a chastened child.

"Okay isn't acceptable either." His body didn't move, but the energy around him shifted. Becoming almost palpable in its force as he stared at her. "Clear communication is essential, Lara. So is honesty. You always have the right to say no, or stop, at any time, and I will honor your choice. But you have to be clear. Yeah and okay imply uncertainty or disinterest, and that does neither of us any justice."

Her nipples ached and she squeezed her thighs together. He wasn't touching her, and his words weren't particularly dirty or sexy, but her body was reacting in a big way to his tone of voice.

Pushing the heady clouds of lust away from her brain she focused on what he'd said. "I can say no at any time?"

"Yes."

"But aren't I supposed to do whatever you say?"

"Only if you want to. That's what makes the power exchange

of D/s so potent. It's a free exchange, one that is meant to give us both what we need."

Need. She nodded, even though she didn't really understand what he was saying. She'd understood she could say no at any time, and that was all she cared about at the moment. *Need* was flooding her pretty damn fast and she hoped he was going to do something about it soon.

Oh hell, he wanted honesty. She licked her lips and leaned forward. "I need you to fuck me, and soon. Is that clear enough?"

Heat flashed through Karl, straight to his cock at her words. "Very good. Shall we go then?"

He slid out of the booth and waited for her. Lara's eyes widened and she stared up at him. "It's as easy as that?"

"It is tonight," he said as she slid out of the booth and stood in front of him.

Karl kept his hand on the small of her back, ignoring the looks as they headed for the door.

Lara was going to get looks wherever she went, for sure, but right then he knew it was the pheromones she was giving off that was drawing attention more than anything else. The heat that *they*, as a couple, were giving off would draw attention even at The Dungeon—it certainly drew attention at that yuppie pub.

When they were outside, Karl glanced down at Lara's pretty face. "Where's your car?"

"I took a cab," she smiled wickedly. "I figured I'd be getting a ride from you."

Anticipation tightened his gut. "Oh, you're going to get a ride all right."

"Perfect."

He led her toward his truck and opened the door for her. When she was in the seat, instead of closing the door and walking around to the driver's side, he stepped in close and put his hand on her bare thigh. "Spread your legs."

Her head snapped around and she gazed at him, her pupils dilated with excitement.

Without a word she parted her knees, watching him as he slid a hand up under her skirt and skimmed his fingertips over her pussy.

So much heat. She was like a furnace, totally hot for him. For what he was going to do to her. "You're so wet, sugar. Are you enjoying this?"

She nodded, and he raised an eyebrow, pulling his fingers away. Before he could correct her and ask for a verbal reply, her eyes widened fractionally and words tumbled from her mouth. "Yes!" she sounded almost panicked. Then calmer, "I'm enjoying it very much."

As a reward, he leaned in, and pressed a quick hard kiss to her lips. "Good girl," he praised, then backed away to close the door.

When he climbed into the truck and started it up she was watching him carefully, and he could almost see the wheels in her mind, shifting gears, sorting things out.

"Would you be more comfortable at your place, Lara?"

"It's close," she said, and recited the address.

He'd planned to have her play with herself while he drove, but instead, he said nothing. He watched the traffic while letting her stew.

She was fighting herself. He knew the signs of arousal, the look in her eyes, the glow in her cheeks, the rhythm of her breathing; she was definitely turned on by being the focus of all his attention. But he had to remember this was all new to her.

Lara was a strong independent woman, and if he wasn't careful, things could end very badly.

He pulled up to the curb in front of a small house and looked at her in surprise. "You live here? Alone?"

"I rent the basement. Graham and his boyfriend, Peter, live upstairs." When she saw his look, she smiled. "It's Peter's house, and don't worry, they leave me alone, mostly. We'll have privacy."

He climbed out of the truck and met her on the walkway. "Are they going to come running when they hear you scream my name?"

She slanted him a look. "You think you can make me scream your name?"

His balls tightened. "More than once, sugar."

Flames leapt in her eyes and she licked her lips. "I can't wait," she murmured before leading the way up the walk to the back door.

Neither of them spoke as they entered the basement suite. Lara kicked off her shoes and waved him in, locking the door behind him. In three steps he stood in the middle of the living room looking around.

There wasn't much to look at. No plants, or personal photos anywhere. Generic pictures of fields of flowers and lakes set in some mountains, a knitted throw spread over an overstuffed sofa, and a twenty-inch TV.

The only thing in the room that hinted at Lara's personality was the laptop on the coffee table and the cluttered bookshelf along one wall. Before he could move close enough to see what type of books interested her, she was in front of him.

"I'm ready when you are." Feet planted shoulder width apart, she thrust out a hip and cocked her head to the side. "Where do you want me?"

Tamping down the hunger that rose shockingly fast, Karl stepped forward and cupped her face in his hands, looking deep into her eyes, searching for what she was really feeling.

Arousal was there, but buried deep he could see a small bit of worry.

9

Karl's head lowered and his lips pressed against Lara's. He started slow and sensuous, his hands roaming over her body, cupping her butt and pulling her close.

"Don't worry, sugar. Nothing will happen that you don't want."

Arousal formed a hard knot low in her belly and she writhed against him, impatient, wanting more. She'd been on the erotic edge ever since he'd walked away from her that first night. He'd interrupted her manhunt at the pub, and as much as she relished the look on his face when she'd walked away from him, her body had hated her for it. No amount of masturbating had satisfied her after *that*.

She clutched at his shirt and lifted a leg, wrapping it around his hip. Closer, she wanted to be closer.

A hot hand landed on her thigh and pushed her leg down. "Slow down, sugar. Show me your bedroom now."

Heart pounding and pussy throbbing, she took his hand and led him to her bedroom. With a flick of her hand, she turned the light on and led him to the middle of the room. She reached out, but before she could touch, he grabbed her hand and pulled her forward, spinning her into his arms. Her back slammed into his front and heat flashed through her.

"For tonight, you don't do anything but get used to my touch," he purred into her ear. "Understand?"

"Oh yeah."

"Excuse me?" He swatted her on the ass.

"I mean yes. Yes, please. Touch me."

One large male hand flattened against her belly, holding her tight to him as the other one inched under her short skirt. "You're a fast learner, sugar. I like that."

Something like happiness made Lara's chest tight, and she puffed out a breath. She wanted to talk, to tell him to hurry up and touch her, to stop being so slow with that hand under her skirt. But she wasn't sure if she was allowed to talk right then, and the last thing she wanted was to have him stop. He felt too damn good.

Then he touched bare skin, and all thought of talking fled. His agile finger tickled over her swollen pussy lips before dipping between them, and Lara's eyes drifted shut and her head fell back against his shoulder. Shifting her stance, she spread her legs and bent her knees, wordlessly begging for more.

Pleasure ripped through her when he immediately answered her actions with a stiff finger thrust deep.

"That's my girl," he said when she gasped and her hips started to roll. "Ride my hand; show me what works for you."

Desire swelled inside her, filling her throat and tumbling out in a garbled expression of need. But she didn't know . . . couldn't say . . . what it was that she needed. A pressure built inside, and she fought the urge to stamp her foot in frustration and instead reached up and popped the snaps on her leather vest, thrusting her chest out.

Karl's hand instantly cupped a breast, thumb and forefinger grasping a nipple and squeezing. She moaned and he squeezed it harder. "You like a little pain there, huh?"

"Yes," she hissed, raising her arms and clasping them behind his neck.

Another finger filled her, stretching her and making her hips jerk as she started to pant.

Her heart was pounding, the sound of blood rushing through her head taking away everything but the sensations flooding her body. The hand between her legs shifted, and another finger was added. She gasped, her fingers digging into his neck as she bore down on that hand. So good, so full. More, she wanted more. His fingers twisted and moved, wiggled and tickled her until her lips opened and words started tumbling out. "More, please, Karl, more, my clit, please, don't stop, my clit."

Everything inside her was focused on the new sensations overwhelming her.

"That's it, baby. Ask for it. Tell me what you need." His hand left her breast and joined the other one between her legs.

Fingers tickled her insides and rubbed her clit as his words washed over Lara. Her muscles trembled; a long, low moan built in her throat, until he pinched her clit and pleasure exploded inside her.

Her eyes flew open and she stared blindly at the ceiling as her body trembled and shook, her knees buckling.

When she was able to breathe again, she realized Karl was sitting on the foot of her bed and she was cradled in his lap.

Holy crap! They were both still clothed, and he'd just given her the best orgasm of her life.

Unable to think—not wanting to think—Lara tucked her head against his neck and sighed, just enjoying the way his hand stroked up and down her back.

"Wow," she finally whispered a minute later.

"Did you like that?"

"Do you really need to ask?"

There was a rumble in his chest; she felt it before she heard it.

"Communication is key, Lara. Remember that."

"Sounds good to me."

They sat in silence for a few more minutes, Lara becoming increasingly aware of the hardness of his cock beneath her butt. Her sex clenched and her nipples hardened.

She'd asked him to fuck her once already. Pride wouldn't let her ask again—not verbally anyway.

She slowly slid off his lap to stand before him. She slipped off her vest and then undid the denim skirt. With a little shimmy, the skirt was on the floor, and she was completely naked.

Without a word, she reached for the snap of his jeans, undid it, when her fingers touched on the tab of his zipper, a strong hand clamped down on her wrist. "What are you doing little girl?"

She raised her eyes to his, but didn't speak. For some reason, she didn't know what to say. When he didn't move or ask again, she licked dry lips and pressed her thighs together.

"What do you need, Lara. Tell me."

She was so empty. Her insides itched and tingled, crying out for him, but the hard look in his eyes said she might not get what she needed. But suddenly she *knew* . . . if she didn't tell him, she definitely wouldn't get it.

"Please," she whispered. "I want you to fuck me."

"You want me to? Or you *need* me to?"

She bit her lip, and the grip on her wrist tightened minutely. She didn't want to beg, but she needed this. She needed *him*.

"I need you," she said, her voice trembling with arousal, and maybe a little a bit of anger. She really hadn't wanted to beg. "I need to feel you inside me."

He smiled slowly, his lips lifting and eyes gleaming as he tugged her back onto his lap. Her hands went immediately around his neck as they kissed. His tongue met hers with such agility that her sex clenched and she ground down on the hardness beneath her.

She wasn't sure exactly what Karl wanted, but submissive

she wasn't. Not if it meant being passive. Her hands went everywhere, over his shoulders, down his back, up his chest. She pulled his shirt off and froze. Awe and desire blended as she took in the sight before her. She'd known he had a tattoo; she'd seen the tip of it. But now she saw it all, and it made her sex clench.

Covering the top of one side of his chest was a big black tribal mark with wicked-looking slashes that curled over his collarbone, up his neck, and over his shoulder. A small patch of downy hair was in the middle of his well-muscled chest, and shiny gold hoops speared through both of his nipples.

Saliva pooled in her mouth, and Lara reached out and nudged one of the hoops, making the light glint off of it. A cross between a sigh and a gasp came from Karl, and her body responded. The primal lust he had inspired returned full force, and she pushed him back on the bed, stretching out on top of him. Her tongue came out, and she licked his neck and nipped at his earlobe while her fingers toyed with his flat male nipples and the jewerly that adorned them. His muscles danced beneath her hands, and she couldn't get enough.

Wiggling down his body, she circled one nipple with her tongue and reached into his pants to free his hard cock. It throbbed in her hand, and she squeezed it gently. The perfect size, long and thick, thick and *hot*. Wetness eased from the head and coated her hand as she stroked him.

"Tighter," he urged her, one of his hands covering hers and showing her how he liked it. "You won't break me, darlin'."

Eagerness swam through her veins, blending with the heat

and need there. All thought fled, making her a purely sexual creature. Soon she had the stroke just right, and his hands slid to her back. One moved up and down in a full-body stroke from tip to tail, sure fingers dipped between her cheeks and then skimmed up her spine. The other hand slid under her hair to cup her head as she worked back and forth between his nipples.

She tongued the little gold hoops, gripping them between her teeth and tugging until he groaned and his hips arched into her.

Need overtook sanity as she arched her back and slid his cock between the folds of her sex. Bracing her hands on his shoulders, she balanced her weight, her nipples rubbing against his as she rocked her hips and felt the hard length of him slip and slide through her wetness.

She rested her forehead against his, eyes locked and breathing his air. Her pussy clenched and she hungered to be filled by him, but the slow and oh so sensual feel of his cock rubbing up and down her slit, nudging her clit with each pass, then nudging her entrance, then her clit . . . Oh God, she was going to come!

"No," Karl commanded softly, his hand in her hair and on her butt tightening, making her freeze.

"Huh?"

"You can't come until I say," he said.

A surprised whimper echoed through the room, and she bit her lip, begging him with her eyes.

He shifted his hips and his cock nudged her clit again. "I need to know how safe you've been."

"Huh?" Pleasure shot through her and she shuddered, her

need overriding everything else she felt. She could feel his pulse throbbing in his cock, right against her core.

"How safe sexually. When's the last time you were tested, are you taking birth control?"

"Yes," she panted. Her hips rocked and his grip on her hair tightened. Pain flashed through her and a rush of arousal dampened them both. "Oh!"

"Lara," he said sharply. "Focus."

She stared into his dark eyes, the fire in them clear. "Yes, safe, tested last month, clean. On the pill."

He thrust up, and a scream jumped from her throat as she was filled. Long hard throbbing cock filled her, in and out, as he pumped his hips fast, lifting her almost off the bed. His hands left her hair, left her ass, both sliding over her ribs to cup her breasts. Every thrust had him hitting her deep, finding a spot deep within her that sent sensation spiking through her body. Her head fell forward, her panting turning into a string of sighs and gasps as she fought for breath.

"Oh, yes. Oh God! Karl!" A scream wrenched from deep inside until she bit down on his shoulder, stifling it as everything in her tightened, then exploded. Lights flashed behind her eyes and she shuddered in his arms.

Her body a boneless mass, she'd just got her breath back when Karl switched his grip to her hips. He thrust deep, holding her tight to him, grinding against her as his cock swelled and throbbed and hot wetness flooded her sex, setting off another small series of pleasurable shock waves.

They lay together, still connected for a few minutes. Lara's brain was fried. She knew she should move, should leave, go get a towel, turn off the light . . . something. But she didn't. She couldn't.

Karl's arms wrapped around her, engulfing her in warmth as he pressed a soft kiss to her temple. "You weren't supposed to come until I said," he whispered.

"I'm sorry," she mumbled. But she really wasn't. The orgasm had rocked her to the core, and she'd loved every second of it.

"Don't be. I'm going to enjoy punishing you for it."

Lara heard the words, and the promise in them, but she didn't care. She just snuggled against him and let erotic contentment lull her into a deep sleep.

10

She looked so sweet, almost innocent, as she snuggled into her pillow. Her mouth was open, and little baby snores escaped every thirty seconds or so as Karl gazed down at her.

He'd eased out from beneath her a while ago, with the full intention of pulling a sheet over her, and leaving. Instead he'd stood, turned off the light, and crawled back onto her bed, where she'd snuggled into his arms.

Lara had eagerness, and a natural capacity for sensation play that he could nurture. But it was more than that. She *was* a submissive.

It was buried so deep inside her, so far behind that wall of independence and attitude that she'd built around herself that even she wasn't aware of it.

But he was.

He must have subconsciously recognized it in her right from the start. It was why he hadn't been able to forget her. Tonight, for just a moment, he'd gotten a glimpse of it.

Karl had seen that her 'do anything once' attitude was just that. An attitude. Sure, she'd back it up, and physically, he didn't think there was anything she wouldn't try at least once. But emotions were a different story. Getting past her walls would be a lot of work, physically, psychologically, and emotionally.

Lara was stubborn and independent. He already knew she'd treat it all as a game, unwilling to admit how strong her need was, even to herself. But that was okay because she *would* accept it, even revel in it, once she was truly his.

Karl's gut clenched and his pulse raced. He should walk away from her right now—she was dangerous. In the space of an hour she'd gone from a potential playmate, to . . . to the one he'd given up on ever finding.

11

Cool air slipped over Lara's skin and she struggled awake. The lights were out and the room was dark. It was the middle of the night and she thought she was alone, until the bed shifted and she realized the sudden chill was from loss of shared body heat.

Scrubbing at heavy eyelids she watched as Karl tugged his t-shirt back on over his head, and sleepy desire stirred within her.

"Where are you going?" she croaked, her voice husky with sleep.

"Home to my place, sugar." His hand smoothed over her tousled hair and he kissed the top of her head. "You were wonderful. I'll call you tonight."

She watched him walk from the room, an unusual type of satisfaction settling in her chest as she hugged the pillow, and closed her eyes. She didn't want to think right then, she felt too damn good.

A sigh escaped as she sank back into sleep. He'd said she was wonderful.

Three hours later, her body heavy with satisfaction, Lara rolled from bed and stumbled into the shower. Not only was there a pleasant tenderness between her thighs as a reminder of the night's activities, but it was also Friday. The perfect way to start the weekend.

The steam built up quick in her little bathroom, and she closed her eyes and washed her hair. She loved to have her hair touched and played with, it was the reason she let it grow long, and Karl had known to pull just hard enough to make her melt.

He obviously knew a lot about what made a woman melt. There was no denying he'd been in charge last night, yet not once had she felt dominated. She'd loved every minute of it. When she skimmed the towel over her body to dry off, her nipples peaked and a shiver danced down her spine. She imagined getting him completely naked and licking him all over.

Lord, the man had a body worth drooling over. And a glorious cock! But she'd been so overwhelmed by sensation that she hadn't even minded that he never took off his pants. Oh yeah, Karl was magic. His voice, his touch . . . yeah, she definitely needed more of that.

A few minutes later, as she was buttoning her jeans, there

were footsteps over her head and she heard the boys arguing—
and she knew what was coming. Grabbing her bag and her keys,
she rushed for the door and managed to avoid Graham's morning
after interrogation. Which was really a good thing because she
wasn't sure she could avoid sharing the dirty details of the night
with them.

Fifteen minutes later, she strolled into the warehouse to pick up
her drop sheet for the day and her truck. Maura, the commander
behind the counter, raised a penciled-in brow. "You're early. And
what's with the perma-grin? You get lucky last night?"

"Did I ever."

Maura's chuckle turned into a coughing fit. "I haven't seen a
smile like that in way too long. Who's the stud?" she asked in her
raspy smoker's voice. "Does he like older women?"

"I have no idea," Lara answered with a grin. "But he likes
this woman, and that's all I need to know!"

The women laughed and Lara got her stuff together and
headed out.

By lunchtime she was having a hard time maintaining her
happy place. Because of that, she chose to get another few deliveries in between twelve and one when most people had lunch, so
she could book off shift an hour early.

Traffic sucked and people were grouchy at the drop offs,
blaming her for being late. The worst came when she had to drop
off some parts at the dreaded garage on Hastings Street. Not that
Hastings was all that bad, but the two brothers who owned the
garage made her skin crawl.

"Oh, look at who came when I called?" The younger brother, Larry, had said when she'd arrived.

"It's the only way women ever come for you, we have to pay them." This from the older brother, Robert.

He spoke with a smile, but it was a mean, malicious smile that never reached his eyes. Not many men bothered Lara, but Robert did. The way he looked at her made the hairs on the back of her neck stand up and her fists clench. It was the same reaction she used to get when her father's drunken friends would leer at her before she'd run away from home.

She held out the invoice. "Just sign here, please," she said, keeping her tone neutral.

"Oh, baby girl, you say please so pretty," Larry said in a voice as greasy as his oil-stained hands.

Lara cocked her head to the side, and stared at him.

Finally he shuffled a little under her stare, looking to his brother for back-up. When Robert ignored him, Larry snatched the invoice from her hand and signed. "You should be nice to me, Lara. You never know when you might need a man in your life."

"It's just business, Larry." She tore off his copy and spun on her heel to leave without looking at Robert again. She didn't have to look to know he was watching her. His stare burned into her, her blood chilling as she let the door swing closed behind her.

The afternoon sun helped chase away the chill in her bones as she climbed into her truck. Spring had definitely arrived. Slipping her sunglasses on, she headed out into traffic, aiming for Taco

Bell for a late lunch. Maybe she should grab an extra taco and bring it back to the shop for Maura. The woman loved fast food, any kind of fast food, even if it was cold.

Her phone rang as she was paying the girl at the drive through and she answered without looking at the caller ID.

"Hello, sugar. How are you feeling today?"

Karl's voice swept in her ear, and straight into her bloodstream. "I'm feeling very fine this afternoon, Sir," she said with a sassy smile he couldn't see. "How are you?"

"Very well, thank you." He paused. "Did you enjoy our play last night?"

"You know I did."

"Physically, yes, you did. Your cunt squeezes nicely when you come, there is no missing it."

His blunt words went straight to her head. For whatever reason, the dirty talk really got her engine revving. "It squeezes nicely when there's a big cock filling it up."

"You like big?"

Heat started to creep up her cheeks and Lara squeezed her thighs together. She felt strangely shy, yet she was getting so turned on too. "I like to feel full."

"Hmm, I'll remember that for next time," he promised softly.

"When is next time going to be? It's Friday night, y'know?"

"Sorry, greedy girl, I have plans for tonight already, for the whole weekend actually, but you and I will get together again soon. Early next week, perhaps, would you like that?"

Would she?

Normally Lara didn't like to plan too far ahead, especially when it came to men and dates. Shit, normally she wouldn't wait either. But, she did want more Karl. "Okay, that'll be good."

"Okay?"

She remembered what he'd said about clear communication. "Yes, early next week will be good."

"I have some homework for you over the weekend. If you do well, I'll reward you."

She snorted, homework? "And if I don't do well?"

"Then you'll be punished." He had *that* tone of voice again. The one that reached deep down and stroked her insides so wonderfully.

Her sex fluttered and her skin tightened. Ignoring the meaning of her body's reaction, she laughed and turned into the warehouse parking lot. "You're just looking for a reason to spank me!"

Karl chuckled on the other end of the line and something fluttered low in her belly. "No sugar, there are better ways to punish you than spanking. In all honesty, spanking isn't a favorite kink of mine. But I'd be happy to oblige you if that's what you crave."

"I crave a good hard fuck, thank you. I don't need a spanking."

Another chuckle, and pleasure warmed Lara. She liked making him laugh.

"Your homework for the weekend is to email me each day— once on Saturday, and once on Sunday—and each email is to contain a favorite sexual fantasy of yours."

"I'm not much of a writer," she said.

"I'm not judging your writing skills. I'm getting to know you." He rattled off his email address and she scribbled it on a napkin. "Be honest with me, Lara, and just maybe your fantasies will come true."

They hung up and Lara sat in the sun for a moment, stunned. These games certainly weren't what she'd expected when he'd said he was a Dom. She was actually enjoying them.

12

Karl hung up the phone and dialed again immediately. "Val, I think it's time for a road trip. Can you get away this weekend?"

"Arghhh!" The aggravated response came through loud and clear.

"What?"

"I don't have a bike anymore, asshole."

Oh yeah, Val's ex-wife had put him through the financial wringer a few months earlier and he'd sold his bike to pay off his club. Now he owned Risqué nightclub free and clear, but that was it.

Women could be so vicious.

He thought about it for a minute. He'd been dealing with divorce negotiations all morning, and his newest client, a nice young thing that had just been dumped by the man she helped put through law school, had literally cried on his shoulder and then asked him over for a home-cooked meal. The meal had sounded good, but the predatory gleam in her eye when she'd voiced the invitation made it clear she wanted to do more than cook him dinner.

He wondered if Lara liked to cook, or more importantly, if she'd like to cook *Him* dinner. There was so much about her he wanted to know. But first, he needed to think, with a clear head.

Glancing at his desk calendar he made a quick decision. "Your birthday's coming up in a couple weeks right? I'll rent one for you, consider it your present. You just get the club covered, and leave the girlfriend at home."

He hung up before Val could argue with him about the plan, and quickly started to call their other riding buddies. Half an hour later, there were a half dozen of them set to leave early the next morning for their first road trip of the year.

A weekend on his Harley, with his buddies, shooting pool and drinking beer was just what he needed. He had a decision to make before he saw Lara again, and he couldn't do it without some serious thought. Being away from the city, away from the office, always helped him remember what was important in life. It wasn't the money, and it wasn't the job.

The job.

Law school had been to make his parents proud, specializing in divorce had been to make money. He'd done that. He now had enough money and investments that he could retire in the next five years if he wanted, and part of him wanted to. Maybe not *retire—*

he'd go insane if he had nothing to do—but the divorce business was getting to him. He knew it. He'd known it for a while now, and being with Lara had truly brought it home to him.

Vibrant and full of life, her tough adventurousness had shown him just how closed up he'd become, and he didn't like that at all.

The road trip was a great idea. He could collect his emails on his cell phone, and encourage Lara so the lines of communication stayed open. He needed her to know she could always contact him, and he needed to see if she would do her homework.

He looked at the clock, and reached for his laptop just as Graham buzzed him. "Mrs. Pollock is here."

"Send her in."

A second later his office door swung open and a classy blonde walked in. Lisa Pollock was in her early forties, slim, and very polished. The perfect society wife—except she didn't like it when her husband cheated on her.

"Hello, Lisa, how are you today?"

"Fine, Karl. How are things going here?"

He explained his last negotiation with her soon-to-be ex-husband's lawyer. "You have the house, and the car, but he's not budging on the alimony. We can take it in front of a judge, and I think we'll win. It's your choice."

"I don't want to take that chance," she said.

She reached into her purse, pulled out a manila envelope, and the hair on the back of his neck stood up. He knew that determined, almost manic look in her eye. He'd seen it before and it was never a good thing.

"Show him those photos and tell him if he won't pay me, I'll show the world." The expensive charms on her gold bracelet jingled loudly in the quiet office when she tossed the envelope on his desk.

Without opening the envelope he picked it up and held it out to her. "Extortion is illegal, Lisa."

Anger flashed across her face, making her ugly for a moment until she got her control back. She picked up the envelope, opened it and held up the photos for him, one by one. "Do you see this? I married this. I worked as a cosmetics saleswoman at a retail outlet for fifteen years while *this* sat at home and played with his paints and made pretty pictures. Now that those pictures have made him worth millions, he thinks he can just dump me. No. Fucking. Way."

Karl stared at the photos she'd flashed, and swallowed a curse. Several curses. He recognized the scene, if not the players. "Who took those?"

"I hired someone."

"Who?"

A calculating gleam in her eyes, she gathered the photos together and slid them back into the envelope. "I'll tell you when I get my first alimony check."

"I'm not giving him that demand," Karl stated. "But I will schedule another meeting. If you need to talk to your husband, I suggest you do it before then."

He stood and walked her to the door of his office, assuring

her he'd let her know when the next negotiation was scheduled. He wanted her there for that one.

Why he was surprised it was going to come down to this he didn't know. Yes, women were vicious, and Lisa Pollock was determined to get more than even with her husband.

Man, he couldn't wait to get on his bike and leave this crap behind for a few days. He needed time to figure out what to do about those photos.

Lara went to bed on Friday night happy with her night's take at the pool tables. There hadn't been any real challengers, just some college jocks eager to believe a woman could never beat them at pool. She hadn't even had to hustle them and after the first few games she'd felt sorry for them.

"All right, guys," she'd said when one of them started to rack for another game when she'd already taken over two hundred bucks from the group. She'd played each of the four of them, and none had even come close to winning. "I'm strictly in this for the money, so why don't you go have a few beers and give someone else a chance to pay my rent?"

She'd been trying to save them from complete humiliation, but they'd taken that as an insult, and wanted to play double or nothing.

She wasn't a complete idiot. If they wanted to throw their money at her, she was going to take it. Because they'd been so eager, she'd hit her goal of five hundred dollars in just over three hours and was home and in bed hours before normal.

Which gave her time to think about Karl's homework assignment.

Her ultimate fantasy had always been sex with a stranger. But she'd lived that out many times in her life already. It was easy to tell herself she enjoyed sex with strangers because she didn't want to get close to anyone, being close to people only invited them to hurt you—or worse yet, to be indifferent to you.

In all honesty, she knew she enjoyed the sex with strangers because she didn't care if they liked her or not, which made it easy for her to not care if they got off. And not caring whether they got off or not made it easy to get what she really wanted, what she really needed, to get off. She could tell them to focus on her clit, to pinch her nipples harder, to not stop.

It was one of the reasons she really didn't expect letting Karl have control to be so good. Normally, if she didn't tell a man what she wanted and how she wanted it, she didn't get it. And here Karl was *asking* her to tell him what she wanted.

Not in person, but in an even more interesting way.

When she thought of it like that, the homework assignment took on a whole new meaning.

Lara got out of bed and went to get her laptop. She was going to do this now. She wasn't going to tell him her wildest fantasies yet, but she would tell him what she really wanted.

She pulled the laptop closer and started typing.

I want to touch you. I want to be able to run my hands all over your body. I want to play with those piercings, and lick, nibble, and maybe even bite at your nipples until you are groaning and begging for more. I want to scrape my nails down your back as you bury your cock deep inside me. I want to dig my fingers into your ass and feel the muscles clench as you pump into me.

Lara looked at the email. It wasn't going to get her published, but what she had there was raw, and real. It was what she wanted. She poised the mouse over the send, and clicked it.

Done.

She closed up the computer and turned out the light, ready to sleep.

13

It was Saturday night, the music was loud, the bar was crowded, and his friends were having a great time. Karl was having an okay time. His restlessness had eased with the five-hour highway ride, but his normal zest for partying was missing. Maybe he was getting old.

"Another beer?"

Karl smiled at the pretty waitress. The makeup she had piled on didn't hide the fact that she was probably too young to be working there, or that she was in no way innocent.

"No thanks, sweetie. Maybe in a little while."

"I see you drooling over her young ass, you old pervert," Val said with a laugh.

"It's a nice ass."

"Too small for my tastes."

"And pervert I may be, but she's too young for my taste." Karl took a swig of his beer and nodded at the bartender who flashed him a finger wave from behind the bar. "Now *she* might be able to get my blood pumping."

"Might?" Val shook his head. "Used to be there was no might about it. You getting old?"

He didn't like hearing his own thoughts thrown back at him. Thirty-six was *not* old. "Discriminating is the right word," he retorted.

He hated to admit it, even to himself, but really, he was just distracted by thoughts of Lara. Her first email fantasy had been okay, but he knew she was holding back. He didn't like that she was still hesitant to really let go with him, even though he understood it. The whole dynamic of power exchange and domination—submission was new to her, and if he was going to pursue the relationship, he needed to help her open up to it more. He had to show her the possibilities.

She'd walked into his life when he'd needed a change, and his instincts told him she could be the one he'd been waiting for. But his brain was telling him she was trouble.

She was independent and strong and way too sassy. He really needed to step up his game if he was going to make this work.

Anticipation swelled inside him. He had plans to make.

"Dawson, man, get with it!"

The raucous call snapped Karl back to the present and he gave his head a shake. He set his beer down and smirked at the guy on the other side of the pool table. "You ready to get your ass kicked?"

Mark, a big bear of man, stood with his arm around some woman he'd been buying drinks for. "Have you looked at the table? You're done."

There were five balls on the pool table; four high balls, and the eight. Karl was high ball.

"I'm not the one who choked on the eight," Karl said as he ambled to the end of the table and lined up his shot.

Down went the eleven, then the nine, then the twelve in a beautiful bank shot that drew praise from everyone but Mark. Karl sent the fifteen to the side pocket, leaving only the shiny black eight ball on the table.

Mark nudged his friend forward. "Flash him your boobs, girl. Make him miss this shot."

Karl glanced up and grinned as the girl lifted her t-shirt and flashed him some breast.

"Very nice," he said, then put the eight ball in the corner pocket. He straightened up with a grin. "But, unlike Mark, it takes more than a little skin to distract me."

Mark patted his new friend on her ass and laughed. "Next time get on your knees, baby. That'll distract him!"

Karl gave up the table and let the others play, his mind wandering to the fact that the thought of that woman on her knees did nothing for him. The cell phone on his hip vibrated just as he sat down next to Val.

He glanced at the phone's screen before flipping it open to greet Marie warmly. "Hey, sweetie, how are you doing today?"

"Hello, Sir, I'm doing very well, thank you."

90

He ignored the knowing smirk on Val's face and focused on Marie. "What can I do for you?"

"You weren't at The Dungeon last night and I was hoping to see you. Will you be there tonight?"

Karl heard the pouty note in her voice and responded naturally. "Are you pouting, Marie? You know I don't like it when my girls pout."

A moment of silence, and he bit back a sigh. "Marie, I'm waiting."

"I'm sorry, Sir. I just miss you. You haven't been around much lately."

She was right, he hadn't been around much. But their relationship was strictly play, and he'd always made a point of keeping it casual. He didn't like her implication. "I'm out of town this weekend, sweetie. I'll be at the club next week, we can talk then."

"Yes, Sir," she said softly.

A twinge of guilt went through him. She wasn't pouting anymore, she actually sounded hurt. He knew what she needed, and he knew he couldn't give it to her. They'd been playing together on and off for a couple of years in an open, casual arrangement, but lately she'd been getting a little clingy. A little too dependent on him. He needed to fix that.

"Marie, you know there are others to play with. I don't want to hear that you're sitting around waiting for me. We've talked about this before."

"Yes, Sir." Her voice was quiet and dejected, and Karl's shoulders dropped. He was going to have to fix this, but he couldn't do it over the phone.

"How about you and I hook up on Monday night? We need to talk."

That perked her up. "Oh, yes, Sir!"

"Okay, sweetie. You go to the club tonight and have some fun, and I'll see you on Monday night."

He disconnected with Marie, and started scrolling through his contacts for Simone, a Mistress who he knew would enjoy some time with Marie.

"So many women, so little time, huh buddy?" Val said with a laugh.

Karl ignored him and headed to the bar to get another beer from the sassy bartender. A little uncomplicated flirting was just what he needed.

All Saturday morning Lara had tried not to stare at her computer. Checking her email was all she could think about, but rushing to do so felt a little . . . desperate. And she didn't like that.

Instead, she went upstairs to get away from the computer and harass the boys for a while. Peter was locked in his office, writing, but Graham played a few games of crib with her. When he finally chased her away just after lunch, she gave in and opened up her iBook.

The mail program opened and she saw a response from Karl

waiting. Her heart kicked in her chest, and she bit her lip. What would he say about her fantasy? Would the Dominant be able to give up a bit of control to her for a while?

She clicked on the email and devoured his response.

Very nice, Lara. I like that you were honest in your needs and desires, but I expected a bit more of a story. Karl

A story? He wanted a story.

Disappointment at his response tickled at her mind for a brief moment before determination stomped it out. She grabbed her keys and made a quick run to the corner store.

Three hours later she tossed the *Penthouse* digest on the bedside table. It wasn't her regular reading material, but she was determined not to make a complete ass of herself with this *homework*. Pulling her computer onto her lap, she opened a new email window. He wanted a story—she'd tell him a story.

Karl,
I'm lying in bed, my hand under my thin nightgown and between my thighs as I think about seeing you again. It's true. You made an impression, and more than ever I want to try everything once. Including anal sex.

As much as I love cock and dream about it, I've not found anyone I trust to introduce me to such naughty delights. But you obviously know your way around a woman's body. And I'm ready for more.

In my fantasy, I'm lying in bed, thinking about you, anticipation making my juices flow steadily. One finger flicks back and forth over my clit, and my eyes close as my other hand travels deeper between my legs until I'm tickling my puckered hole.

Tiny flutters of sensation run though me, and I dip a finger into my pussy, swirl it around, and get it covered in juice, then bring it back to my ass.

Unable to help myself I push my finger past the tightness and thrust it as deep as I can. A soft moan escapes my lips into the empty room as I wiggle my finger around inside. An idea flashes behind my closed eyelids and I pull my hand away.

Leaning over I open my bedside drawer and search until I find what I'm looking for—my small silver bullet vibrator. I lube it up and lie back with the remote in one hand and the bullet heading for my back door. Knees spread wide, I press the phallic bulb against my anus. Holding it there, I turn it on to the lowest speed and the tingles of pleasure that ripple through me make me gasp your name. You like it when I call your name, don't you?

I want more. I want to slide it inside me, let my ass hug it tight and feel those wondrous vibrations from deep inside. But stories of people having to go to the emergency room to have things removed from their asses make me think twice. Where are you? I want you to do this, to help me. I want to roll over, get on my knees and elbows for you, and have you breach my virgin hole, but you're not here.

I lie there, playing the egg around my puckered hole and frigging my clit with my finger, but I can't get off. I just sit on the edge of an orgasm, ready to scream.

Finally, giving up, I turn it off and go to put it back in the drawer, and my fingers brush against a foil packet. A light bulb goes on inside my head and excitement floods me.

I rip open the condom packet and slide it over the bullet. Lying back in bed I reach between my legs and start playing again.

This would work. The vibrations are still strong and the trailing end of the condom insures I'll be able to get the bullet out, in case the electrical cord breaks.

Impatient for it all, I press it against my hole slowly and it slides into me easily.

The small egg is inside me completely and the vibrations radiate through me. Turning the speed up a notch I begin frigging my clit. Within seconds my belly tightens tellingly and my hips press harder against my finger. Every time I thrust my hips against my flickering finger my insides clutch around the tiny vibrator in my ass. Before I can catch my breath, my orgasm hits and I'm crying out loud, my whole body tensing as waves of pleasure wash over me.

I'm so exhausted by the powerful orgasm that I just switch off the remote and doze for a bit, the egg still inside me.

The touch of soft lips against mine brings me slowly awake, and I realize you've let yourself into my place. I don't mind, in fact, I open my arms and welcome you back with a deep kiss.

"What's this?" You pull away from me, holding up the remote for the egg in your hand.

You tug it lightly and notice the cord dipping below the covers. When I try to reach under the covers and retrieve the egg you grab my hands and stop me. With a wicked grin, you flick the button and the muffled hum of the vibrator fills the air, and my juices immediately begin to flow.

"Thinking of me, huh?" you say as you pull the cotton sheet lower and order me to bend my knees and spread my thighs. When the sheet is past my knees you see exactly where the egg is, and your grin widens.

"You're such a dirty girl."

I blush as you dip a finger between my thighs and feel how soaked my pussy is. I am a dirty girl. I want so much, I want to do it all, I want to do everything—to have you do anything to me.

"Oh, baby," you whisper in that husky voice that makes my insides melt as you step back and strip off your clothes. "You don't know how happy you've made me."

Soon you're naked, your cock waving in the air, pointing at me like a "dirty girl" radar and making me drool. Wasting no more time or words you pull me out of bed and bend me over so my hands are braced on the mattress. You tug on the condom hanging out of me like a tail, and the egg pops out of my exposed anus. A tiny moan escapes my lips.

Your large hands grip my ass cheeks and pull them apart. My breath catches in my throat, I know what's coming next.

Sure enough, the head of your cock nuzzles at my entrance. Gently, but firmly, you ease into my asshole. It's almost painful, the stretching of my virgin territory, but it feels oh so good too as you slide in inch by luscious inch.

Once you're in to the hilt, we both let out slow breaths. I giggle and you groan. Then you start to move and my breath disappears once again.

God! You feel huge! Pleasure swamps my entire being as you start to pick up speed.

"I can't hold back," you say as you pound into me.

I don't want you to wait, I want you to lose control because I feel so wild with you. I'm whimpering in pleasure and urging you on like a porn star. "Oh, yes! Fuck me, Karl! That's it!"

I push back against you and slip a hand between my spread thighs. A small tap on my swollen clit, and my whole body spasms in orgasm.

My body clenches around you and you cry out, your hot come filling up my insides in a whole new way.

My trembling knees finally give out and I fall forward onto the bed, you on top of me, and still inside me. Our hot breaths mingle as you kiss me gently before slipping off me and onto the bed.

Lara

14

Karl adjusted himself in his chair and snapped his cell phone closed. He'd told her he wanted a story, and she gave him a story all right. Pleasure and excitement raced through him, side by side. With only slight encouragement, she'd exceeded his expectations.

Lara was turning out to be quite the eager girl with real desires that grabbed him by the balls. He stared at the light layer of sweat that coated the palm of his hand. He really wanted her.

"So who is she?"

"Who's who?" Karl opened the menu and skimmed it briefly before setting it aside.

Val turned in his seat and eyed him.

It was Sunday morning and they were sitting next to each other in the roadside diner at Grand Forks Junction, their last stop on the weekend road trip.

All six men were seated around the table laden with eggs, sausages, bacon, pancakes, and toast, loading up before getting on the road and heading home. But with six men, there were so many conversations going on no one was paying attention to them.

"It wasn't a work message because it made you smile. Put that together with your surprise visit the other night, and the fact that you didn't pick a woman up all weekend and I know you've got something going on. Spill."

"It's nothing I want to talk about."

"Bring her by the club when you're ready," he said before placing his order with the waitress.

Bring Lara to Risqué? The idea had appeal. He'd love to see what Val thought of her.

But first up, he wanted to see what she thought of The Dungeon.

15

Sunday morning Lara was kicking her own ass for sending her second email to Karl the night before instead of waiting until morning. It sucked that she had no way of knowing if he'd even read it yet. Or worse, what if he read it right after she sent it and since it had been Saturday night—*late* Saturday night, but still Saturday night—what if he thought it was another attempt at the first fantasy and he was expecting another one for Sunday?

No. He'd said two emails, she'd sent two, that was good enough.

All morning she stewed about Karl's reaction to her story. Her computer was plugged in and she checked her email obsessively, waiting for his response while she did laundry, washed dishes, and tried not to imagine him reading the email and bursting into laughter.

She'd told him she wasn't a writer. He better be happy with what she'd sent. Checking her email file one more time she saw that he still hadn't responded. UGH! This was nuts. She wasn't submissive, she didn't even know what submissive was! Why she'd agreed to give this a try was beyond her.

It was the challenge. Sure, she wanted a safe, sane, normal life. She really did. Her childhood had been enough of "different" to last her a lifetime. But safe and sane also meant finding other ways to keep life from being too boring. And a straight-out challenge from a supersexy man that made her pussy clench was one way to do it.

When Lara was seventeen, after two years of scrounging, stealing and running, she'd met Richard. Richard had been in his midtwenties, a good guy who'd found her sleeping in an alley one night and offered her his couch. After a month on his couch without him trying to get anything from her, she'd realized he really was a good guy. For whatever reason, he'd wanted to help her.

She'd slept with him then. Given him her virginity and pretended to be his girlfriend until she could find a job, and get out on her own. They'd both known what was happening, and they'd both been okay with it.

He'd introduced her to the pleasures of her own body. Although he'd never been able to give her an orgasm, it had been good. In all honesty, the only time she orgasmed during sex was when she took charge.

Until Karl.

Excitement zinged through Lara. Maybe there really was

something to this submissive thing. Her curiousity piqued, she typed DOMINATION SUBMISSION into the Google search engine and stared at the results.

Holy shit!

Links to articles and websites dedicated to kink filled the page and Lara grinned. Oh yeah, it was definitely time for her to see what this was all about.

Picking a link, she clicked on it and was instantly rewarded with the view of a simple, yet classy-looking site. Lara looked at the photos in the website header, all black and white pictures of women in various poses of submission. One woman was naked except for a black leather collar, another was bound with a rope that circled her breasts, immobilized her body, and framed her pussy. There was a back shot of a woman bent over, a crop pressed lightly against her bare buttocks.

A minute trembling starting inside Lara as she studied the photos. They were explicit, but not pornographic. They were beautiful and highly erotic . . . and when she read the quote beneath them, an involuntary shudder rippled through her.

I want to live darkly and richly in my femaleness. I want a man lying over me, always over me. His will, his pleasure, his desire, his life, his work, his sexuality the touchstone, the command, my pivot. I don't mind working, holding my ground intellectually, artistically; but as a woman, oh, God, as a woman I want to be dominated. I don't mind being told to stand on my own feet, not to cling—all that I am capable of doing but I am going

to be pursued, fucked, possessed by the will of a male at his time, his bidding.
—*Anaïs Nin*

Pursued, fucked, and possessed by the will of a male.

A delicious shiver ripped through Lara and she squeezed her thighs together . . . and read more.

A couple of hours later, Lara was a little overwhelmed. The technical terms, etiquette, and safety rules had been enlightening, but the most engrossing stuff had been the sex blogs she'd found.

People who lived the lifestyle, or just enjoyed the kink as a part of their life, spilled everything on an anonymous journal for anyone to read and comment on. And read she had; she'd even commented on a couple, asked questions, and gone back later to discover that they'd been answered.

Lara was amazed at the openness, and the sincerity of the words from people she'd never met.

She bookmarked one in particular to read more of later. She'd already scrolled back and read posts from the woman who'd struggled with her fantasies of rough sex and pain and humiliation, before she'd found the man who accepted her, and gave her everything she needed.

SubbieDreams blog brought Lara to tears at one point, and turned her on so much she was squirming in her seat at others. She might not want the pain and humiliation that woman had craved, but the closeness, and the open acceptance she'd found seemed magical.

Okay, so maybe a bit of the rough sex stuff appealed to her. Being tied up and having Karl touch, tease, and test her to see exactly what got her off could be a lot of fun.

The scary part was that in all of the personal accounts and sex blogs, the submissives talked about never holding back, about open and honest communication. She had no problem with that when it came to sex, but she wasn't so sure she'd ever be capable of completely letting a man into her head.

It just wasn't safe to let anyone get that close.

The timer on the oven went off and she used a tea towel to pull out the casserole dish. Homemade macaroni and cheese, yum. Enough to feed her and the boys on their Sunday movie night.

She set the hot bowl on the counter to cool just as there was a knock on the door.

Since when do the boys knock? Shit, since when do they go outside and come around to the door instead of using the stairs and the inside entrance by the bathroom?

She tossed the towel on the counter and answered the door to a face full of flowers.

Stunned, she just stood there and stared.

"Delivery for Lara Fox," came the muffled voice from behind the flowers.

Footsteps trampled behind her and Graham squealed. "Ohh, gorgeous flowers!"

He jostled to get past her. "This is Lara, I'll take those for her. Lara sign for them, dear."

Lara signed the page on the clipboard the guy held out and closed the door with a smile. "Thank you."

She turned and watched as Graham shuffled over to the kitchen table, oohing and aahing over the big bouquet the whole time. Feeling a little lost, Lara stood glued to the spot.

She'd never gotten flowers before.

Peter came over and put an arm around her shoulders, urging her forward. "Your birthday's not for another couple of weeks, so what did you do to earn flowers?"

"There's a card."

"Give me that." Lara jumped forward and snatched the card from Graham's fingers. No way did she want him reading it. The flowers had to be from Karl.

She opened the little envelope and pulled out the card.

Very nice story. Well done.

That was it. Five words and no name.

But her chest tightened and her insides warmed just the same.

"Well, who are they from?"

"Graham," Peter muttered.

"What?"

"Don't be so nosy."

"Puleease, as if she's not gonna tell us anyway."

"They're from Karl."

She fingered a pretty orange and brown flower. It was a big

flower, the whole arrangement was huge. And so colorful. Orange, white, pink, red. She didn't know what a lot of them were, but she recognized the giant colorful daisies, and there were roses and some sort of lily too.

"Oh, honey, I should've known," Graham looked at her, his brow wrinkled with concern. "Are you okay?"

"Of course I'm okay. They're beautiful." She laughed.

"But, Lara honey, they're kiss-off flowers." Graham looked at her, then the card she still held in her hand. "Aren't they?"

"No, why would you think that?"

Graham looked from Lara to Peter, who was ignoring them both and pulling plates from the dish rack where they air-dried. "He always sends his female clients flowers when their case is over. It's his standard thank-you and good-bye."

Lara shook her head. "Not this time. Never mind that I'm not a client, but the card is more of a . . . thank-you than a kiss-off."

"But—"

"Graham," Peter interrupted. "Shut up about it already, and come and get some dinner. Have you seen *Pirates of the Caribbean* yet, Lara? We brought one and two down for movies tonight."

Hurt flashed across Graham's face at Peter's tone and Lara stilled. It wasn't like him to be so harsh. Usually it was her telling Graham to shut up or back off.

A small ache formed in the pit of her stomach.

Was there trouble in paradise?

16

Monday morning wasn't anything special. Typical slow start for the brain, with everything else around Lara going at warp speed. Just after lunch, her phone rang on her hip and the sight of Karl's number on the caller ID slowed everything to a crawl.

She flipped her phone open and tried to sound casual. "Hello?"

"Did you like the flowers?"

"What's not to like? They're gorgeous. Thanks."

"You earned them. That was some fantasy you sent me. I thought you said you weren't a writer?"

"I'm not. Maybe I'm just a pervert."

His affectionate chuckle echoed over the phone line and a shiver rippled through Lara. "I like that about you," he said. "I'd like to take you out tomorrow night. To a special club."

Tomorrow? She'd already waited all weekend, full of hormones and fantasies. Yet, she found herself agreeing to wait another day. "Okay. What time?"

"I'll pick you up at nine. And Lara?"

"Yes?"

"Wear a skirt for me again, with no panties."

Butterflies came to life in her belly and her nipples tightened. "Ohh, it's going to be a naughty night out, is it?"

"That will really depend on you," he said. "See you at nine o'clock."

Lara could swear she floated above the ground for the rest of the day. Part of her knew she was letting herself expect too much from Karl. Shit, it was only their second date, and she never saw a man more than three times . . . so it was going to end soon. But she was determined to enjoy it while she could. That attitude was what had kept her sane.

The Dungeon was pretty quiet on Monday nights, which is why he'd planned his visit for that night. He had a few things to accomplish, first off being a visit with the owner.

"Mr. Hardin, Thanks for seeing me tonight." Karl held out his hand to the clean-cut man standing behind the desk.

"Not a problem, Karl. Please call me Mason. Valentine Ward spoke very highly of you. He also said you had something I really need to know about?"

He'd had a hard time getting a meeting with the mysterious

owner of the club, so he'd had Val give him a call. Being the owner of one of the hottest nightclubs in town, Val had been able to set up the meeting as a favor.

Once they were both settled, Karl got straight to the point. "Someone's taking compromising photographs of your members, while they're within The Dungeon."

As a lawyer, and a Dom, Karl was pretty good at reading people's expressions, but Mason didn't give anything away. A breach in security like that would mean the club's business. Members of The Dungeon paid highly to be able to play in a safe, protected environment. "And you've come by this information how?"

"I'm sure you've read my membership file, so you know I'm a divorce lawyer. One of my clients is going through a bit of a nasty one, and she's procured some photos of her soon-to-be-ex-husband as leverage. She refused to tell me how she got them, but I will find out. I just figured you could work it from this end as well."

The muscle in the club owner's clean-shaven jaw twitched. "You saw the photos?"

"Yes."

"Describe them."

"To be blunt, a pretty well-known male client, strapped to a padded horse bench in the Shared Room with a dildo shoved up his ass and a cock down his throat."

Suddenly Mr. Clean-cut didn't look so calm. "The Shared Room," he said. "Do you know when they were taken?"

Karl shook his head. "No, and I'll do my best to make sure my client doesn't use them, but I think you'll need to do some damage control there anyway."

Karl stood, and the two men shook hands. "Sorry I had to bring this to you, but we both know how important it is."

"Yes, thank you," Mason said. "It'll be dealt with, and quickly."

Karl left the office and put that issue in the back of his mind.

Second up was a chat with his mentor and friend, Simone, before Marie arrived. Mistress Simone was a friend. A beautiful, sultry Latin woman with a well-rounded body that looked illegal in black leather. They'd probably have a helluva good time in bed together if they didn't kill each other, but both would fight for control . . . so instead, they worked scenes and subs together every now and then. She was someone he trusted to tell him if he was being a complete idiot.

"Simone, thanks for meeting me tonight," he said to the raven-haired beauty he found already seated at his favorite booth.

"You know I'm always here for you, Karl. Especially when you're so generous with your playmates." She winked at him. "Your little Marie is a treat."

He smiled. Perfect. "I'm glad you enjoyed her, but she's not strictly mine. She can play with whoever she chooses."

"Really?" Simone tapped a red-painted fingernail on the tabletop. "She gave me the impression that she was strictly yours when I suggested we get together again."

"Did she give you a hard time?"

"Oh, no, she was delightful to play with, and very polite when she said she'd be happy to please me, *anytime you instructed her to.*"

Karl waited while the waitress set their drinks on the table with a small smile. He'd been afraid Marie was getting too attached. Her phone calls and the fact that he'd not seen her play with anyone else at the club for a few months had made it clear it was time for him to do something.

"I'm going to tell Marie tonight that I won't be playing with her anymore," he said when the waitress was gone and they were alone again. "She might need some attention."

Simone's eyebrows rose. "You've been with her for a while, haven't you?"

"Almost a year," he nodded. "But I made it clear from the start that it was a play situation only. While we have taken it outside of the club, it's been scene-play only, and I've never offered up a collar. She knows I play with others and I've encouraged her to as well."

"But she hasn't?"

"Only when I've arranged it."

Simone nodded, her dark eyes serious as they looked at one another. Karl didn't need to say any more, he knew she understood his worry. "Is that the only reason you're turning her loose? You're feeling pressured?"

He took a swallow from the frosty beer in front of him before answering. "You are entirely too astute at times, Simone."

"I am good, aren't I?"

They chuckled and he met her gaze. "I've met someone I think could be special."

"Do I know her?"

Karl shook his head. "She's not part of the scene. In fact, she's not even aware of her own submissive nature."

Simone's eyebrows jumped. "How did you meet her?"

"It was a random meeting. We had dinner, and I thought that was it. She's loud, bold, and even brassy, so I walked away. But I couldn't get her out of my head, and when I saw her again, she showed me something rare. She feels . . . *right* when I'm with her. Like she was made for me."

"Does she know what you are?"

"I've told her and, adventurous minx that she is, she's willing to give it a try. But I don't think she truly understands what she's getting herself into and . . ."

"And what, baby?"

He blew out a breath and met her gaze. "And I'm not sure *I* know what I'm getting into. But I can't walk away."

"Then don't," Simone said simply, laying one of her hands over his. "You've been playing and skimming the surface with these playmates of yours for a long time. Now it's time to get serious. You go after what you want, and maybe you'll both find what you need."

He nodded. What she said not only made sense, it had a ring of truth to it that he couldn't deny. He'd just been coasting, playing. It was why meeting Katie Long had affected him so deeply. She'd wanted more than play.

Simone patted his hand on the table. "I'm here if you need me for anything."

"Thanks, Simone."

She grinned at him wickedly. "And it'll be my pleasure to ensure little Marie doesn't miss you in the least."

They laughed and Karl felt some of the tension ease from between his shoulders. Marie would be there soon. He'd say good-bye to her in one of the private rooms, with Simone there to cushion his departure.

17

Karl bit back a growl on Tuesday night when Lara opened the door and he saw what she was wearing. Anticipation had been building inside him all day. Every minute of free time his mind had filled with ways to introduce Lara to her true nature. But none of that had prepared him for the sight of her again.

The leather vest from the other night had been lovely on her, but this . . . this was a totally different kind of Wow.

He'd been expecting another tight showy number, not the one-piece dress that skimmed from the curve of her breasts to the top of her thighs. It looked like she'd gotten out of the shower and wrapped a thin black silky towel around her body before stepping into knee-high black leather boots.

"Wow," he said.

She smiled. "You said a naughty night, so I'm ready for action."

His blood heated, and his balls filled. So was he.

But first, "Lift your dress and show me how well you listen."

Her eyes twinkled and she tilted her head, making the thick dark hair sway across her shoulders. "You said no panties. I was a good submissive and did as you asked."

The words were right, but the twinkle in her eye said she knew exactly what she was doing. She was testing him.

"Show me," he commanded.

Lara stopped a foot away from him. Far enough away that he'd have to reach to touch, but close enough that her scent tickled his nose. Her full lips tilted and she lifted the hem of her dress without hesitation.

Karl's breath caught when he saw her pussy. Not only was she pantiless, she'd shaved. Completely.

"Very nice," he said, fighting the urge to touch. "Did you do that for me?"

"I thought you might like it. I like it." She reached between her thighs and touched herself. "So soft, and very sensitive now. Even the breeze when walking is a turn-on."

Get a grip, buddy. His mouth watered and his fingers tingled. He wanted to touch, to taste, to delve between the thick lips and seek out all her hidden secrets.

Instead he just arched an eyebrow. "Did I say you could touch?"

"No."

"Then stop."

Her hand pulled away and she dropped her dress, her eyes glued to his expectantly. She was waiting for something from him.

He held out his hand to her, and when she laid hers in it, palm against palm, he pulled her close. He kept hold of her hand, and lifted his other to cup her cheek and stroke his thumb over her full bottom lip. "Tonight, you can ask anything you want, say anything you want, but you're to *do* only what I say, okay, sugar?"

Her pupils dilated slightly and he heard her breath catch. Then she nodded, her grip on his hand tightening slightly.

He pressed a soft kiss to her mouth and stepped back. "Good girl." He gestured to the door and she sashayed through it.

Lara locked up the house and he took hold of her hand again, intertwining their fingers as he led her to his truck. He'd toyed with the idea of using his bike, but he'd asked her to wear a skirt and it wasn't quite warm enough to have bare skin on the windy road.

"So where are we going?" she asked as soon as he climbed in and started the truck up.

"The Dungeon. It's a private club I belong to." He swiveled his head and met her gaze. "One that will help you to understand what I want and expect from you. And what you can depend on from me."

"What about what I want from you?"

"We'll cover that too." He bit back a smile. She was quick.

"I did a little research on BDSM and this Dom thing, and I have to say, some of it sounds too good to be true, while other aspects of it are pretty scary."

He'd planned to just sit and talk with her for the first while once they reached the club. He wanted to let her get a good look around while they talked about limits and safety and got comfortable. He should've expected Lara wouldn't wait for explanations from him. She took life head-on and full speed ahead and this was no different.

The streetlight ahead of them turned red and Karl slowed the truck to a stop. When he glanced at her, she was watching him closely.

"Tell me what you learned," he encouraged her. "And always feel free to ask me anything."

"How many submissives do you have? Do you top men as well as women? What's my safe word going to be? Are you just into the bondage and discipline, or the sadomasochism thing too?"

A bark of laughter jumped from Karl's mouth before he could bite it back. When he saw her brow snap forward he immediately leaned toward her. "Come here."

She leaned in and he kissed her. Soft, slow and sensual, just touching his tongue to hers before pulling back. The car behind him honked and he started forward again, the light green.

"What was that for?"

"I wasn't laughing at you. Your knowledge and questions

surprised and pleased me. The kiss was a thank-you for asking them."

"Oh."

"I'm what's known as a loving Dom, or a gentle Dom. I'm not into large amounts of pain or humiliation, and those I play with don't often require it from me. I believe in the reward and denial system of training." He flicked his eyes from the road to her quickly. "But make no mistake, I *will* punish you if you disobey."

He saw her nod, her mouth twisting slightly. "So this is more than just a 'do anything once' game. You're interested in training me?"

There was an empty parking spot almost directly in front of The Dungeon and Karl pulled into it, turning the truck off before he turned to face her, his pulse racing.

"I don't want you to think of it as training, not yet anyway. For now, I just want you to think of it as an introduction to your true nature. No!" He put a finger against her mouth when she started to interrupt him. "I know you don't believe me, and that's okay for now. I'll earn your trust."

He could see the gears in Lara's head turning. Her eyes brightened and little white teeth nibbled at her bottom lip.

He reached out and stroked his thumb over that lip soothingly. "You always have a choice, sugar. For tonight, you can watch only, or you can be involved. But if you say yes to being involved, then you are *mine*. I have complete control of what you do and what happens to you. You will submit to me and my desires. Understood?"

She nodded once, and Karl's pulse raced while he waited for her answer. He was right to give her the choice now. If she said yes, then it was the last choice he was giving her. "Do you want to decide now? Or go inside and check things out a bit first?"

Flames leapt to life in her eyes. "I understand, and I don't want to just sit and watch. I'm yours."

Pleasure washed over him and he let her see a glimpse of it. "Very good. You can always ask me anything, but do not disrespect me by talking back, or balking at my commands. You asked what your safe word would be?"

Lara nodded, her eyes bright and nipples visibly hard through the thin material of her dress.

"You don't get one. Forget about what you read or what you've heard and concentrate on what you *feel*. I'm in control, and you must trust me to be aware of what you need and to give it to you." He took a deep breath and felt his own hunger stir. "I can smell your excitement, Lara."

He felt the shiver that rippled though her and she met his gaze. "Yes, Sir."

Adrenaline coursed through Lara's veins. She felt like she was on a ledge, and below her was an abyss. A very tempting and beautiful abyss, that was full of unimagined pleasures.

Karl helped her step down from the truck and kept hold of her hand as they approached the club entrance. He led the way down a set of stairs and past the huge linebacker of a doorman who held the door open. There was another set of stairs, narrow ones that lead them down into the underground club. With each step Lara became aware of the steady throbbing music, and the way her pulse seemed to match it, becoming heavy and languorous.

At the bottom, there was another bouncer, and this one greeted Karl by name. "Good evening, Master Karl. Your booth is ready for you, and Julie will be serving you tonight. Is there anything else you'll need, Sir?"

"Thank you, Josh, but I think that will be all for tonight."

Karl kept his fingers entwined with hers as he led Lara through the club at a leisurely pace. He exchanged nods and smiles with a few people, but he didn't stop as he made his way to the back wall. Lara tried to be casual about all she was seeing, but she was sure her pounding heart could be seen clearly by everyone in the room.

The Dungeon had chains and manacles hanging from the walls, and the dimness of the cavernous room had a blue tinge to it that made it warm, yet a touch surreal. People were dressed in various styles. Some wore casual street clothes, others were topless, some were in full leathers, and a few looked like they'd stepped directly out of the erotic photos she'd found on the Internet.

Lara knew she looked good, but a sudden exhibitionist streak had her wishing she'd worn a thong so she could strip off the dress and strut.

As soon as that thought entered her mind, an older man wearing leather pants and a vest with silver studs walked by holding a leash. On the other end of the leash, walking a step behind him was a plump woman wearing nothing but the collar attached to the leash, and a silver chain that hung between her pendulous breasts, clamped to each nipple.

"Here, sugar." The humor was rich in Karl's voice as he directed her to slide into the circular booth he'd stopped at. She met his gaze as she slid across the cushioned seat and couldn't hold back her delighted grin.

"This place is amazing. How come I never knew it was here? I play pool at the pub directly across the street and I never even noticed it."

"Maybe you're not as observant as you think you are?"

She smacked him in the arm playfully and went back to looking around the room hungrily. The place had a very different feel to it for her. She was always comfortable in bars, she'd been hanging out in them since she was ten years old, but this didn't feel like just a bar. It felt . . . electric.

Her heart was pounding, her blood was racing, and her thoughts were slowing. Feel, Karl had said to just *feel*.

When a pretty girl in a black leather bra and tight leather pants that laced up the front stopped in front of their table, it took Lara a moment to notice the small name tag pinned to her waistband, and realize she was the waitress.

Julie asked Karl what they would like to drink and left to fill their order without a word spoken to Lara.

Indignation swelled at being ignored and she tensed. But before she could speak, Karl laid his hand along the back of the booth, and his fingers gripped the hair at the base of her skull tightly.

He turned her head so she was facing him. "I ordered you a juice," Karl said, as if he could read her thoughts. "Remember, you are mine, Lara. Trust me to take care of you. That includes ordering your drink."

Their gazes locked for a tense moment as Lara realized just what she'd agreed to. A knot of arousal curled low in her belly and she automatically lowered her gaze from his piercing one. Once her gaze was lowered, Karl's grip loosened and his fingers massaged the back of her head.

Sensations swamped Lara. Pleasure, anger, fear, and arousal. How could she feel so much at once? All brought forth by a man she barely knew.

She gave herself a mental headshake and straightened her spine. She could do this. She could do anything.

"Look at me, Lara."

He could've easily made her look at him again. His hand was still buried in her hair, it wouldn't have taken much. But the command was in his voice, not in his touch, and that is why Lara raised her eyes to his once again.

Karl's eyes were dark whirlpools that sucked her in. She could feel her doubt and insecurities flow from her at the clear confidence in that gaze. The strength in that hand wrapped in her hair was not there to hurt her but to guide her.

"Yes, Sir?"

The words floated from her lips naturally, and everything in her softened at the pride and pleasure that filled his gaze. His lips tilted and his eyes closed in a slow lazy blink that made her pussy clench. "Come sit closer to me. I want your hand always on my thigh unless I say otherwise."

Lara shuffled closer, her hand reaching beneath the table and eagerly settling on the muscled thigh that now brushed against her bare one as Julie arrived with their drinks. Karl called her his while she was there, and it gave her comfort to know that he was hers as well.

Julie smiled and left the table just as another female caught Lara's eye.

She looked almost like a pixie with short wispy hair that framed her face and a small diamond flashing in her nose. Her tight body was shown off to its best in a white fishnet body stocking, with only a scrap of silk wrapped around her hips sarong style. But something about the way the woman walked had Lara's nails digging into Karl's thigh.

No, it wasn't her walk, it was the way her eyes were zeroed in on Karl as she sashayed right up to their table and slid into the booth on his other side.

"Hello, Master," she said and put her hand on Karl's other thigh.

18

Lara's hand started to slide off his thigh when Jan sat down, and Karl turned his head to look at her, a warning clear in his voice. "Lara."

Her hand stilled and her gaze left Jan to focus on him. Temper was clear in her bright blue eyes, but it was tinged with a bit of doubt. Leaning forward, he pressed a kiss to the corner of her mouth. He didn't want her having doubts. "Lara, this is Jan. I want you two to get along."

He turned to greet Jan, who'd been waiting patiently like the good submissive that she was. He pressed a soft lingering kiss on her lips and smiled into her pretty grey eyes. "Jan, sweetie, this is my new friend, Lara. She's my guest, and it's her first time here. I want you to be her friend, okay?"

His choice of words wasn't lost on Jan. Her eyes widened, before she lowered them briefly. "Yes, Master."

"How was your day today, sweetie?" He made small talk with Jan for a few moments, stroking his fingers through Lara's hair the whole time. He wanted to give them a few moments to get accustomed to each other while he was in the middle, then he'd make the next stage of the night clear to them.

Karl could tell by the tension in Lara that she didn't know what was going on, but Jan was fully aware of the importance of Lara being his guest.

Jan knew he'd never brought a date to the club before. Normally, he showed up alone, played, and occasionally extended an invitation to certain playmates to his home.

That made Lara special.

Fortunately, he'd been playing with Jan on and off for a couple of years and knew she had no intention of trying to settle down with him. Jan enjoyed the sexual games and was a bit of a pain slut, but he wasn't the one for her, and they both knew it. It was why they were so good together when they played.

After a few moments of silence, Karl's hand stilled in Lara's hair and he spoke clearly so they would both hear. "I've booked a private room for us tonight, ladies, but it won't be ready for another hour. So what I would like right now is for you, Jan, to take Lara on a tour of The Dungeon. Show her everything, and answer all of her questions."

His fingers tightened warningly in Lara's hair and he leaned forward to speak in her ear. "Jan is a good girl and has known me for years. You can ask her anything about me, our play together, and the lifestyle, but you do so with respect. She's earned it." He pulled back and met her gaze, showing her how serious he was. "You understand?"

The pulse in her throat throbbed, and he saw her swallow before she nodded.

"Good girl." He put his lips to hers and gave her a long slow kiss, his tongue slipping between her lips and tasting her until she moaned and softened against him.

"Jan, sweetie. You be a good guide and I'll reward you well." He patted her thigh softly before giving it a small but vicious pinch.

Her cheeks flushed and a bead of sweat popped out over her lip. "Yes, Master," she said in a breathy voice.

"Good, you girls go become friends now."

Karl watched the two women slide out of the booth and look each other over for a moment before Jan gestured Lara forward. Lara flashed him an unreadable look before turning and walking away. He let out a slow breath.

He wanted to be the one to show her around, to introduce her to the place, to the rooms and the people. But he knew it was better this way. He had to remember not to smother her, or coddle her. That wouldn't do either of them any good.

Lifting his beer, he took a slow swallow and looked around the club, letting his thoughts wander. He knew Lara was anxious to be fucked good and hard, and if she behaved well, he might reward her at the end of the night. But before that could happen, he needed her to understand that while joking and being sassy had its place when they played, he was the boss.

Her "do anything" attitude thrilled him, but he needed her to be sure she understood what it encompassed when she said "Yes" to him. Excitement settled in his gut. Tonight she'd get a look at exactly what he was capable of.

He took another drink of his beer when Jan took Lara down the hallway that led to the Shared Room and he lost sight of them. He wished he could be there when she saw the public play. He knew it would make her little exhibitionist heart flutter.

The hair on the back of Karl's neck stood up and he tensed. He was used to stares and looks but this felt different. Someone wasn't just looking at him, they were *watching* him.

The crowd shifted and he saw Marie sitting at the bar. She smiled at him and waved her fingers. He smiled back and nodded. Their talk had gone better than he'd anticipated the night before. He'd told her that he'd done a lot of thinking and he felt that he wasn't enough for her. She was sweet, beautiful, and loving, and she deserved someone who could fill her needs better than he could.

When she lifted her drink from the bar and moved in his direction Karl stifled a groan. He'd known her easy acceptance the night before had been too good to be true.

"Hello, Marie," he greeted her.

"Hello, Master." She came to a stop at the edge of his table and he deliberately did not invite her to sit.

"You don't need to call me Master anymore, Marie. We're just friends now. How are you?"

Something ugly flickered across her face, but it was gone so quickly he wibdered if he'd imagined it. "I'm doing well. I was just getting ready to leave for the night and saw you sitting here. I thought I'd say hello, to show you there were no hard feelings."

He smiled. "Thank you, Marie. I appreciate it."

When he didn't say anything else and still didn't invite her to sit, she smiled graciously and set down her empty glass. "That's it for me tonight. I have an early shift in the morning. Have a good night, Sir."

"Be safe, Marie."

He watched her leave and wondered again at the complexities that make a person who they are. Marie was a strong, forceful, and independent officer on the city police force, who thrived on being sexually used and occasionally punished.

It almost seemed that the stronger the bottom was in their vanilla life, the deeper their submissiveness ran when it came to their sexual self. He glanced up, saw Simone heading his way, and relaxed, thinking Marie must've met with her earlier.

19

Lara was surprised when Jan took her hand and led her through the club. Neither of them spoke, and Lara's confusion grew. Sure, she'd told Karl she'd try anything once, but where in her fantasy emails did it mention another woman? She should've known. Men always wanted more than one woman. He never had answered her question about how many subs he had.

"So . . . Karl said you've known each other a few years?" She asked the blond pixie in fishnet.

"Yes, I met him here, and we played together several times before I was ever invited to his home." Jan met Lara's gaze steadily. "And even then, it's always been only scene-play with us. Master Karl is a good Dom, one of my favorites, but he's always made it clear this is all there was for us."

"This?"

"Sexual play. If he ever decides it's time to stop playing with me, I'll still welcome him as a friend."

Lara digested what she'd heard as Jan led her down a short hallway.

"The Dungeon rents private rooms for play, as Master Karl has already stated, but this is the Shared Room for when those rooms are booked, or for those who like to have an audience."

"Wow!" Lara forgot all about the fact that Karl had invited another woman to be part of their play that night when they entered the Shared Room.

A well-dressed male and female stood in the middle of the circular room, watching the action in each separate cubical that surrounded them. The male nodded to Jan as she led Lara slowly around the room.

"There is always at least two staff members in the room to monitor play and make sure that everything that is happening is consensual and nobody is pushed beyond what they can handle." Jan spoke softly. "While furniture, towels, and cleansing wipes are provided by the club, the members have to bring their own toys. Master Karl has a few favorites he keeps in a locker here, and you'll find he's a man with a wickedly creative imagination."

"I like imagination." Lara grinned and tore her gaze away from the cubicle in front of her where a shirtless man had a naked woman blindfolded, bent over a padded bench, and tied down. Even from where she stood, Lara could see the dildo in the woman's ass and see the excitement leaking down her thighs as her butt clenched and released against the vibrator. The steady slap of leather against her buttocks seemed to add to the woman's pleasure.

The raw scent of sex permeated the room. Lara took a deep breath, letting it soak into her system. Her blood felt thick, her limbs heavy as she turned and watched a woman in four-inch heels flick a riding crop against her male bottom's nipples. He was strapped to a big X Cross, naked except for a spiked harness that circled his testicles, spikes turned inward. "Ouch," Lara murmured.

Jan followed her gaze. "Am I right in assuming you're new to all of this?"

She really didn't want to admit to this beautiful woman that she was feeling just a bit overwhelmed—a woman who already knew Karl more intimately than she did—but Karl had said honesty and communication were key, and all the websites and information she'd read reinforced that.

So she straightened her spine and met Jan's gaze. "Yes, I'm completely new to all of this."

A delighted grin spread across Jan's pixie face and she started pulling Lara from the room. "Then you've seen enough of this, let's find a corner and talk."

After a quick stop at the bar, where Lara grabbed a juice and Jan a bottle of water, they parked themselves at a small table opposite the row of booths where Karl was still sitting. Lara was happy to see he was by himself, just lounging there looking both arrogant and yummy.

"Hey, Lara, wipe the drool from your chin, and pay attention. We only have another twenty minutes or so before we need to get back. Tell me how you met Master Karl, and how you got him to agree to train you."

She was so open that Lara couldn't stop herself. She opened her mouth, and the story of her first meeting with Karl spilled out. Then the story of their second meeting.

"Oh my God!" Jan's jaw dropped. "You sucked his cock in an alley and then walked away from him? Are you crazy?"

Lara laughed, "Yeah, I think I'm crazy to have agreed to this. Come on, Jan. We've known each other—what? Forty-five minutes? You're going to tell me *you* think I'm good submissive material?"

"Why do you think you're not?" she countered.

"Because I'm not too interested in the pain and humiliation stuff." She covered her sudden insecurity with a shrug and a wink. "But the being tied up and touched all over seems like it could be fun."

"Why do you think that appeals to you?"

"Because it's all about me, baby. I'm no virgin, but I've never met a man who could put a woman first like that. To touch them, tease them, play with them. Make them come until they begged you to stop? Oh yeah, that appeals to me big time."

"You know, not all of us are submissive in our every day vanilla life either. If you're not truly interested in exploring this side of yourself, why are you here?"

She shrugged. "I told Karl I'd try anything once. He took me up on it."

Jan eyed her. "There's more to it than that. But that's okay, you don't need to tell me everything. Master Karl knows what he's doing, and I trust him. Do you?"

Did she? Karl seemed like a pretty decent guy. She sure didn't think he was going to hurt her. That was trust, right? "I trust him."

"Okay then, let's go. We need to get back to him. I'm not looking for any punishment tonight. Speaking of which, I need to conclude your tour." Lara followed as Jan stood, talking a mile a minute as she led the way back to Karl, pointing out things as they went. "That's the stage. Occasionally The Dungeon has theme nights or workshops on anything from spanking to edge play. There are ladies' rooms, there and there, the second one also being a locker room with locks for storing toys, or a change of clothes, and showers. The main bar is there and a small one over there, and that doorway leads to the upstairs, where the private rooms are."

They were less than ten feet away from Karl's booth when Jan finally ran down and Lara bit back a smile. The tour was complete, and she was eager to see what was next.

20

When they got upstairs, there was another well-dressed bouncer at the top, blocking the hallway to the private rooms.

"Are you over eighteen?" The bouncer asked Lara.

Surprised, she grinned. "Oh yeah. Thanks for asking though, babe."

His lips twitched. "And you know what happens in these rooms?"

Huh? Lara turned to look at Karl, who stood behind her and Jan on the stairs. He just met her gaze with a small smile and a slow lazy wink that raised her temperature. She turned back to the bouncer. "Yes, I know what the private rooms are for."

"And you're entering them willingly?"

"And I'm entering willingly. Eagerly even." She grinned.

He stepped back and let her pass. Jan and Karl followed her

without being questioned. Karl led the way down the hall, past two other doors, before stopping and unlocking one. He sent her and Jan in, and Lara was surprised to see it didn't look like, well, like a dungeon. Instead, it looked like a bedroom. A very lush and decadent bedroom, but still a bedroom.

Deep burgundy walls, hardwood floors with several plush area rugs here and there, and dark hardwood furniture. A bench seat, a club chair, and the extremely large bed that was set against the back wall. The bed definitely dominated the room.

Lara was so engrossed in searching for an X cross or some sort of bondage equipment that she almost missed the security cameras in each ceiling corner.

"Disappointed?"

"Not at all. Just surprised." She turned to see a small smirk on Karl's face and shook her head. "What was that at the top of the stairs?"

"The Dungeon is a private members club. Members all have signed waivers on file, but guests like you don't. It's just a legal precaution."

Karl walked over to the bed and set down the small satchel he'd brought in with him. Lara saw that Jan followed him, head up, eyes down, always just a step behind him, and she felt a twinge of possessiveness.

When he turned from the bed and ordered Jan to strip and stand at readiness, Lara was quick to step up beside her. "Lara, sugar, you sit your butt on the edge of this bed and wait your turn."

Lara watched as Karl unzipped the satchel and started to remove various toys and things. She recognized things like nylon rope, a dildo, a couple of butt plugs, wooden clothes pins, and a flogger. Her skin tightened and her pulse raced. She shifted on the bed, hyperaware of the shift of the energy in the room.

"Sit still, Lara," Karl commanded.

She lifted her eyes to his face and saw him watching her. "Yes, Sir," she murmured.

When he turned to Jan, Lara's gaze followed, and she swallowed hard.

Not three feet away, Jan stood completely naked, feet spread two feet apart and hands laced together behind her head. Her nipples were hard and flushed red against her fair skin and, as Lara's gaze skimmed over her, she bit back a gasp at the piercing visible between Jan's swollen pussy lips.

Karl walked over to Jan, a length of white rope in one hand. He ran the other hand over her rib cage, down to her hip. When he repeated the same move with the ends of the rope, a visible shudder went through Jan.

Karl started murmuring to Jan. Lara couldn't hear the words over the soft music coming from the corner speakers, but his tone was soft, yet commanding. He wrapped the rope around Jan's ribcage, just under her breasts, then tied a knot between her breasts, and then wrapped it around her again. This time over her breasts. Then over her shoulders, and down between her legs, and through them and up the center of her torso to be tied off again.

Envy shot through Lara at the sight of the rope spreading Jan's pussy lips open. It was crude, but oh so beautiful, at the

same time. Lara's own sex tingled and she pressed her thighs together, flexing her inner muscles.

She flexed again and pleasure started to build low in her belly.
Her eyes slid shut and she concentrated on her inner muscles, her
juices flowing and orgasm building.

"Lara!"

She started, her eyes snapping open to see Karl frowning at
her. "Stop it."

What? How did he know what she was doing?

She saw his frown deepen and she sat up straighter, and
smiled at him. "Sorry." It didn't matter how he knew—he *knew*,
and that was enough.

He walked toward the bed and her heart started to pound,
only to stutter to a stop when he just picked up another length of
rope and went back to Jan.

Why was she even there? Karl had asked her if she wanted
to take part and she'd said yes, but here she was sitting on the
bed while he tied some other woman up. Not that she wanted to
be tied up herself, but . . . well . . . maybe she would. Jan's body
was flushed and her eyes closed, the expression on her face one of
serene pleasure as Karl wrapped the rope around her wrists.

Being tied up didn't look so bad.

Karl raised her bound wrists and did some more tying. At
a murmured command from him, Lara saw her try to pull her
hands back in front, but she couldn't. Jan's feet were still flat on
the floor, legs spread, but with her arms like that, her torso was
stretched out and completely open.

Lara could certainly see the appeal of the position. And she tried not to notice the jealousy that started to creep into her system when Karl began to circle Jan, his hands skimming over her breasts, tweaking and pinching nipples, and smacking her on the ass.

"You have a lovely ass, Jan, but it looks so much better when it's all flushed and pink." Karl lifted his hand and smacked her again.

"Yes, Master."

Lara's pussy clenched, and she tore her eyes from Karl's hands to watch Jan's face. Her eyes were closed and her mouth open as she breathed out with each fall of Karl's hand.

After a few smacks, Karl stepped up behind Jan, his gaze meeting Lara's over Jan's shoulder as he reached around her, cupped her breasts, and pulled roughly at her nipples. "Open your eyes, Jan, and see how Lara's watching you. See the hunger in her eyes? Lara likes to have her nipples played with just like this too."

Mesmerized by the sight of Karl's hands on the other woman, the music from the club faded, the furnishings of the room faded, and she focused completely on the couple in front of her. She licked her lips and shifted in her seat, crossing her legs and flexing her inner sex muscles as she watched his strong fingers work those big red nipples.

"No," Karl spoke loudly. "Lara, uncross your legs, sugar. Spread your knees apart and lift your dress so I can see how juicy you're getting."

Lara lifted the hem of her dress and spread her legs. Cool air floated over her hot sex and a shiver ripped through her.

She watched as he tugged Jan's nipples out until Jan gasped

and arched forward. "Oh, yes, I like to hear those little sounds you make," he purred. "Do you want more, sweetie?"

"I want more," Lara said eagerly.

"I'm glad to hear that, sugar." Karl's voice was pure seduction as he met her gaze over Jan's shoulder. His hands not moving on Jan's breats. "Jan, I'm not going to ask you again."

"Yes, Master," Jan gasped. "Please. I want more. I want whatever you'll give me."

"Take off your dress, Lara, and stand in front of Jan."

Lara wasted no time. Her expensive silk dress hit the floor and she reached for the zipper of her boot only to stop at Karl's command. "Leave the boots on. I like them."

Eager to have Karl's hands on her once again, she stood in front of Jan. "Mirror image, Lara," Karl said. "Whatever my hands do to Jan, I want to see your hands doing to you."

Impatience flared and Lara opened her mouth, only to snap it shut when she saw Karl's blond brow lift expectantly. He was expecting her to fight him.

Determined to prove she could do this, she brought her hands up and cupped her breasts. He pinched Jan's nipples, Lara pinched her own. He tugged at Jan's, and Lara pulled at her rigid nubs until she couldn't bite back a small moan at the arrows of pleasure that were shooting from her nipples to her sex, hitting every nerve in between.

"That's a good girl," Karl encouraged as one of his hands left a breast and traveled over Jan's belly to spread her pussy lips open crudely.

Keeping her gaze locked on Karl's, Lara skimmed a hand over her belly, over her smoothly shaved pussy and spread her slick lips with two fingers. A whimper escaped when his other hand followed and she saw him flick the silver hoop that pierced the hood of Jan's clit.

She kept her eyes on his finger as she kept her pussy lips spread, and started to rub her own hot button. It was hard and covered in juice and Lara's insides immediately started to tremble. She started to pant as she watched Karl work Jan's clit. He didn't slip a finger in, or deviate; all the attention was on the nerve center and both girls were panting, their breathy moans and sighs filling the room to the point that Lara almost didn't hear Karl's voice.

"Lara, stop."

"What?" Her eyes snapped up to his, her chest heaving, her finger poised on top of her throbbing clit.

"Remove your hands from your body *now*."

Not even trying to stifle her whimper, Lara's hands automatically followed his command and dropped to her side, clenched into fists. "But why?"

"Because it pleases me." He kept his eyes on her as he turned his head and spoke into Jan's ear. "Come for me, sweetie."

Jan's eyes rolled back in her head and her mouth opened in a keening cry as her body trembled and her scent permeated the air between them.

Lara's body screamed in protest and her anger swelled. *She* wanted his hands on her. *She* wanted to come. Why didn't he let *her* come? She'd done everything he'd said!

"Good girl, Jan." He pressed a soft kiss to her cheek and urged her toward the bed. "Sit down on the bed for a minute, sweetie."

When he turned to Lara she faced him silently. She was scared if she opened her mouth she'd say something really bad and he'd make her leave. His hands circled her waist and he pulled her close enough to press his forehead against hers.

"I want you to think back to the other night when I was playing with you." Karl met her gaze as he spoke, his eyes like pools of liquid chocolate. "Remember when I told you not to come until I said it was okay?"

Oh, yeah.

"I said I was sorry," she whispered.

"And what did I say?"

"That you would punish me for not listening later."

"That was a very small punishment, Lara." His hands slid to her ass and he pulled her hips flush against his. His hard-on pressed against her belly and her sex clenched hungrily. "You need to always do as I say, trust that I *will* give you what you need. Understand?"

"Yes, Sir."

He kissed her then, his lips covering hers and his tongue swooping in to conquer hers before he pulled back and nipped her bottom lip. Then with a sharp slap on the ass he told her to get on the bed with Jan.

"Okay, girls, let's have some fun." He peeled off his t-shirt and walked over to the toys he'd spread out when they entered the room.

21

He'd had a brief mental outline of how he'd wanted the scene to play out before he'd even picked Lara up that night. And it had played out better than Karl had expected.

Lara was not shy about her needs at all, and throwing Jan into the mix hadn't shaken her up for more than a moment. Satisfaction flowed steadily though him as he took in the scene the two girls made on the big bed. He could've taken Lara to his house and invited Jan over. It's not like Jan had never been there before, but he'd guessed that just being in the club would ramp up Lara's desires and he'd been right.

What he hadn't anticipated was how deeply her eagerness would affect him. His cock was rock hard and his jeans uncomfortable, but the discomfort didn't compare to the pleasure of having Lara accept her lesson like a good girl.

Zoning in on his toys, he picked up the riding crop and the red jelly vibrator before instructing Jan to lie on her back across the width of the bed. "Knees bent, feet planted on the mattress by your ass." Then he had Lara stretch out in the same position, but the opposite way. "Arms above your heads, Lara, the same way Jan's are tied. There will be no touching yourself, you are here for *me* to play with."

He walked to the edge of the bed and looked down at Jan's pretty fur-covered pussy. The little blond curls couldn't hide the flushed state of her engorged cunt. It was wet, shiny, and pink. He leaned forward and slid a finger inside her.

She moaned and Lara's head turned. "Stay as you are, Lara. Watch in the mirror on the ceiling if you want, but do not move."

Jan's sex smell was becoming heavy and he saw Lara's nostrils flare as she watched his movements in the mirror above. He added a finger to Jan's hole and pumped it in and out slowly a few times, judging her readiness. When he was thoroughly coated with her slippery juices, he pulled his fingers out of and eased the vibrator into her.

"There you go, baby. Doesn't that feel good?"

"Yes, Master," she said.

He straightened up and enjoyed the view for a moment before lifting the hand with the riding crop and, with a flick of his wrist, bringing the tip of it down on Lara's left nipple, making her body jerk.

Before her surprised cry had faded he tapped it again, and then the right nipple.

He alternated light taps between her nipples until her chest was flushed and a light sweat had broken out on her forehead.

Up and down, light little taps, he watched her muscles twitch and listened to her. She didn't speak, but her cries of surprise, passion, and occasionally pain, were music to his ears. He alternated them from her nipples to her thighs, and over the underside of her arms raised above her head. Her cries grew increasingly louder, and her body was soon arching into the snaps instead of away from them.

When he pulled the crop away and snapped it over Jan's nipples, Lara's mewl of distress blended with Jan's pleasure and it went straight to his head. He needed to hear more.

Stepping a little closer to the edge of the bed, he concentrated on one of Lara's nipples. Circling the nipple he tapped the side of the breast, the under curve, and all the plump flesh around the nipple, then he switched to the other breast, and did the same thing until they were both a bright pretty pink, the nipples rigid and deep red.

Completely fascinated by the way her skin tightened and flushed so quickly he went to work on her inner thighs again . . . until he tapped the crop directly over her clit and watched her body arch up and her eyes widen in panic.

"Do not come, Lara," he warned her, tapping her clit repeatedly. "You can't come until I tell you or I'll have to punish you again."

"Yes, Sir." Her eyes were no longer watching the action in the mirror, but glued to him. He saw the pulse throbbing in her neck, and watched her hands twist together above her head, as she reacted to the steady tapping of the riding crop.

He watched her jerk and angle her hips into it, then away, into it again, then away as moans and whimpers escaped from her mouth. Her hands shifted on the bed, inching toward his leg, where her fingers touched his thigh. He met her gaze, looking down at her pretty face, flushed and contorted with her effort not to come, and he couldn't say no. "Come for me, Lara."

Her hands gripped his legs, fingertips digging in as her eyes closed and her body arched in pleasure. Karl lost himself in the sight. She was so beautiful, so greedy and eager at the same time. Sweat trickled down his own forehead and he unsnapped his jeans and ran his thumb over the swollen head of his cock. He could come right that second, just from watching her. Even better, he could walk around to the other end of the bed and bury himself deep while her cunt was still spasming. That tight massage would send him to heaven and back within seconds.

"Master, can I come?"

Jan's cry brought him back to the present and he cursed. He'd never gotten so lost in one girl that he'd forgotten the other before!

"Ask me again, Jan," he commanded hoarsely.

"Master, may I come?" Her voice shook and he bent down and twisted the knob on the vibrator again. "Again."

"Master!" Her panic was clear now. "Master, may I come? May I come, Master!"

"Yes." He leaned forward and sucked on her clit, tonguing

the small hoop there as she shattered around the vibrator, completely aware of Lara's hand still stroking up his thigh as he did.

When Jan's body stopped shaking he pulled back, kissed Lara on the lips, pleased when she didn't flinch from Jan's flavor. He stroked her hair back from her forehead and looked down into her eyes. "You're such a beautiful girl," he said.

Her hand shifted up his thigh and she cupped his balls. "Fuck me now?"

He grabbed her wrist, pushed it away, and stepped back. *Fuck!*

Sucking in air, he reached deep for his control. "Get on your hands and knees."

He moved around the bed and bent over Jan's head. He kissed her lips and looked deep into her eyes. Her breathing was good, her color was good, and she was smiling.

"Are you hungry, sweetie? You've been so very good tonight, you deserve a treat."

Jan's eyes gleamed and she nodded. "Oh, yes, Master. She looks delicious."

"Okay, get behind her and start licking."

He stepped back and looked at Lara's naked up-tilted ass and the view of her shiny wet vulva before him. He swung his gaze to Jan and watched her struggle to get up from her position on the bed, knowing that she enjoyed every minute of it. When she was on her knees behind Lara, he unbound her wrists and reseated the vibrator inside her, shifting the rope between her thighs to hold it in.

"Good girl, Jan. This is your reward, sweetie."

He walked over to the club chair a few feet away and sat down facing the girls.

Lara's eyes met his, her surprise clear. She'd expected him to fuck her when he'd said to get in that position.

"Not tonight, sugar." He shook his head, not letting her see his regret. "You let Jan enjoy your pussy for as long as she wants while I watch."

Shifting in the chair a bit, he spread his thighs in an effort to give his balls some space. Christ! He was harder than he could ever remember being, and all he wanted to do was bury himself deep inside Lara and enjoy the feel of her coming apart around him.

He stared at her mouth, her bottom lip caught between her teeth as she tried not cry out at the attention of Jan's pierced tongue buried between her thighs. He could shove his cock down her throat while Jan ate her, but that would still be a step in the wrong direction.

It would be giving in to her hunger for him. And if he did that now, he'd never get control of her. He needed to build her need for sexual pleasure into a need for *Him*—then he'd feed the need.

Like the need in her eyes right then was just to come, but it wasn't necessarily for him. "Come for me, Lara. I want to watch you come."

Her eyes popped wide, and she started to pant. Seconds later she threw her head back and her cry of pleasure echoed through the room.

"Again," he told her. "Come as many times as Jan can make you, but you are not allowed to move from that position."

Lara's cheeks flushed, her bright eyes meeting his as she moaned and another orgasm hit. If it weren't for the faint pleading look in her gaze, he'd take her stare as a challenge. But her challenges weren't as bold as that.

No, she wouldn't challenge him directly after agreeing to give being submissive a try. Lara was too proud for that. The pleading was for him; he could sense that it was starting to happen. The orgasms were good, but that look told him she wanted him, and he needed that.

She probably didn't even know she *was* challenging him.

Karl knew it though. He knew better than to let a sub touch him without invitation during a scene. First he'd forgotten about Jan, then he'd let Lara touch his leg, grip his leg. Sure, she was eager, but she was greedy too.

Damn it, he *knew* that. Her actions demanded he get tougher on them both. That he not only control her, but himself also.

It was a first.

Jan was the first to recover when Karl called a halt to the playing. She came out from behind Lara, who collapsed on the bed after coming more times than he could count, with a dreamy smile on her face.

Pride filled his chest as he got up and walked over to the bed. They'd both done very well tonight.

First he checked on Lara, whose eyes cracked open when he brushed back her hair to see her face. Her pupils were fine and her breathing was deep and falling into a regular pattern. He pressed a kiss to her damp temple. "Sleep for a little bit, sugar. I won't leave you."

Lara's eyes drifted shut, and he leaned over Jan, who had curled up on the bed next to them. Using a towel he'd taken from the stack in the room's private bath moments before he called the stop in play, he wiped her face clean, stroked her hair and kissed her gently. "You're such a good sub, sweetie. Did you enjoy yourself tonight?"

Jan's lids fluttered open and she smiled at him. "Yes, Master. Very much."

"You know you're very special to me, don't you, Jan?"

"Yes, Master."

Warmth filled him and he made sure she saw it in his expression. "This will be our last time together for a little while."

Jan nodded slowly, understanding clear in her gaze. "She's special isn't she?"

"Yes, I think she is. But she needs a lot of training and all of my attention for now."

"Yes, Master."

Karl began to undo Jan's ropes, the silence between them both comfortable and poignant. When the ropes were all removed, he settled on the bed, a hand on each naked woman as they dozed lightly, content with his decision. About fifteen minutes later, Jan stirred and rose from the bed.

After quietly dressing, she leaned down and kissed Karl good-night. "If she needs someone to talk to, you can give her my email," she whispered. "Good luck. You deserve to find *the one*."

The door opening and closing as Jan exited the room was not loud, but it was enough to wake Lara up.

"Hey, sugar," he greeted her when she focused her heavy-lidded gaze on him. "Ready to get cleaned up?"

Lara hummed her compliance and he stood, holding his hand out to her. He led her to the private washroom and had her stand by while he turned the shower on. A few quick twists on the knobs and he had the temperature right.

He unzipped Lara's boots and helped her ease her feet out.

"I can walk," she protested when he picked her up to put her into the shower.

"I know," he replied. "But I want to do this. And what I want goes."

He knew he was taking the after care a little far for the relatively simple scene they'd just had, but he couldn't stop himself. The need to take care of her, to cuddle and touch and clean and pamper, was too strong.

After a very brief inner struggle, he ditched his jeans and climbed into the shower with her.

"Oh, yes," Lara murmured, running her hands over his chest, then reaching for his semi-hard cock.

"No, Lara," he said sternly. "This isn't play time. Let's clean you up, baby."

Irritation flashed across her expressive face, and he waited, but she kept silent. When it was clear she wasn't going to speak, he smiled and kissed her forehead. "Good girl."

He soaped up his hands and skimmed them over her body. Cupping her breasts and making her spread her legs so he could wash her pussy and inner thighs.

A small whimper sounded when he stroked across her clit and he crooned to her. "I know, baby. You're very sensitive now, aren't you?"

Like a needy little girl, she curled up against his chest and his heart skipped a beat.

She was the perfect fit.

The water streamed over them for another minute before Karl shut the taps off, wrapped her in a towel, and carried her to the bed. The sensual haze was fading from her eyes and she was watching him silently as he toweled off and got dressed again.

He picked up her dress, and held it out to her, watching carefully as she silently put it on. He set her boots down in front of her and quickly put his toys away.

"C'mon, sugar. Let's go home."

He put his arm around her shoulders and led her through the short maze of hallways above the club, until they exited the building at street level. His truck was five feet away and he helped her in, buckled her up, and was behind the wheel before she spoke.

"So," she said. "How'd I do?"

He glanced at her quickly, pleased to see her eyes were alert and awake, even though she was relaxed back against the seat while she watched him drive. He grabbed her hand and put it on his thigh with a small squeeze. "You did great."

A comfortable silence fell, and Karl tried desperately to ignore the way Lara's thumb rubbed tiny circles on his thigh. His hard-on had finally gone down and she had his balls tightening all over again.

But there was no way he'd tell her to stop. Not then.

He pulled up to the curb in front of her house and turned the truck off, but before he could climb out of his seat, Lara's hand squeezed his thigh. "You stay here, Sexy. I can make it in on my own."

He froze and turned to look at her. "I will walk you to the door and make sure you are home safe."

Her eyes widened and he saw her walls quickly rebuilding in her mind. "Sure, okay," she said with a shrug.

He climbed out of the truck and walked around to her door. The night was dark, the neighborhood quiet, and all he heard was the blood rushing through his head. Did she have to start testing him again already?

He helped her down from the truck, grabbed her hand, and led the way to the separate entrance at the rear of the house for her basement suite.

His cock was rising fast, and the need to pin her to the wall and show her who was in charge was one he would not deny. The second Lara pushed open the door he moved.

He had her pinned to the wall with his body pressed full length against her. "I am the one in charge, Lara. Not you." He pressed his forehead to hers and stared into her eyes, willing her to accept his words—his will. "If I want to walk you to the door, I will. If I want to spank your ass, I will. If I want you to bend over and take it up the ass, you will. Do you understand?"

Blue fire lit up her eyes at his words, and her breath rushed out in pants. "Yes, Sir."

"Say it."

"You're in charge."

She said the words, her excitement visible in the rapid pulse at her throat and way her body strained against his, but there was still a defiant spark in her eyes.

Karl slammed his mouth down on hers, parting her lips and thrusting his tongue in deep. He ground his hard-on against her sensitive pussy until her hands were clutching at him, her leg lifting to wrap around his hips, her whimpering cries filling his mouth.

Then he pulled back. He sucked on her full bottom lip for a second and then scraped his teeth over it. "Sweet dreams, my girl."

And he left, closing the door behind him and leaving her propped against the wall. He should've told her she couldn't masturbate without his permission, but he forgot.

22

She couldn't sleep. The crisp cool sheets rubbed against her sensitized skin with every breath, and her mind would not shut down.

It still amazed her that Karl hadn't fucked her. Sure, she'd had a good time with orgasms galore, so many that she'd lost count, and passed out as soon he'd called a stop to Jan's attentions. The woman really knew how to eat pussy, her tongue piercing adding a certain edge to the experience—but it hadn't been a cock.

That was the problem with women for lovers. After living with her father and dealing with his drunken friends all the time, her opinion of men hadn't been very good. It had been so bad that she'd thought she was a lesbian. She'd *wanted* to be a lesbian . . . but it hadn't worked out that way.

The gentle touch of a woman was pleasant, and she'd yet to

meet a man who could eat pussy as well as another woman, but Lara loved cock.

She loved the weight of a man on top of her, the feel of him touching, rubbing, and inside her. How sick was it that she'd suffered her dad's friends' creepy stares and sneaky touches until one of them had gone too far and she'd finally fought back—yet the thing that turned her on the most was the feeling of a man's body invading hers? Or having him in control of her body, and God, that orgasm-on-command thing! She'd never been an easy O, but when Karl told her to come, her body clenched and shuddered with sensation.

He invaded her senses without even touching her.

There were times when just the tone of his voice made her cream her panties, his scent, the piercing gaze . . . he seeped into her from every direction whenever she was close to him. He made her forget that it was just physical. He got into her head and used it to pleasure her body.

He hadn't even touched her when they were in that private room. She'd touched herself, while he watched. He used a riding crop to touch her, and, ohh, it had felt good. The sharp stinging snaps of pleasure had zinged from her nipples to her sex, and from her sex to every nerve in her body.

That had been an all-new experience for her. One she'd thoroughly enjoyed. The role-playing had been intense, and the tender care afterward had been . . . unique.

Diluted arrows of pleasure zipped from her nipples when she flopped onto her stomach and they scraped against the sheet. A smile curved her lips and she buried her face into the pillow. She was okay with him having control of her body when he made it feel so damn good.

Lara's eyes popped open and she sat bolt upright in bed. A quick glance at the clock told her she'd slept through her alarm and was late for work. Adrenaline flooded her system and she jumped from the bed.

Since she'd been so deliciously washed the night before, she didn't bother to shower. Mind in total lockdown, and an untoasted strawberry Pop Tart clenched between her teeth, she locked the door behind her and made the dash for her car.

Graham, dressed in a lime green shirt that was so bright it hurt her eyes, yet somehow managed to look good on him, was just climbing into his silver Mitsubishi and he slapped her ass as she jogged past. "Late night, Lara?" he called out with a smirk.

Lara ignored him and kept moving around her car only to stop dead in her tracks. "Fuckin' bitch!"

"Hey!" Graham cried out. "I was just teasing."

She threw her hands up in the air and glared at him. "Not you. This! Did you see this?" She pointed at the tires on her car.

Both tires on the driver's side were completely flat. The rear tire had a jagged slash in it, and the front tire had a big black knife handle sticking out of it. Her phone was already in her hand when she realized she'd been about to call Karl. Why the hell would she call him?

She clipped the phone back on her hip, and then bent down to pull the knife out only to have Graham snatch at her hands. "No! Don't touch it. The police will want to see it."

"The police?"

"Well, yeah." He stared at her. "This wasn't an accident, honey. You need to call the cops."

"Now?" Then she'd have to wait around for them. "I don't have time for this, Graham, I'm going to be late for work."

"What's going on?"

Peter was padding down the driveway, barefoot, with a steaming mug of coffee in hand. Lara's mouth watered.

"Look at this. Graham says I need to call the cops." She pointed to the tires before reaching for his coffee mug and taking a drink. She grimaced at the taste, but took another, hoping the caffeine would help clear the fuzziness from her brain.

"It looks like you pissed someone off," Peter said, accepting his coffee mug back automatically.

"What? You think this was directed at me personally?"

Peter gestured up and down the road, his green eyes serious. "Do you see anyone else with a knife sticking out of their tire? Not to mention the fact that they left the knife behind. I'd see that as a threat or warning of some kind."

A shiver danced down Lara's spine. "Whatever. I haven't done anything to anyone, so it was probably a case of mistaken identity."

Peter reached down and pulled the knife from the tire and examined it. "Good knife too."

"Shouldn't we have left that in, for the cops?" she asked. Just in case it *had* been meant as a warning to her.

Peter put the knife in his other hand, the clank of the steel blade against his ceramic coffee mug a chilling sound. He saw her shiver and wrapped his arm around her in a half hug. "The police won't drive out here just to see a couple of slashed tires. You can report it by phone if you want, or I can do it for you."

"How do you know for sure?"

He smiled and squeezed her shoulders. "You learn all sorts of trivia when researching for fiction novels."

Suddenly, Lara became aware of Graham's silence, and the way he was watching her and Peter. She met his gaze and raised his eyebrows. *What?*

He shook his head. "C'mon honey, let Peter make the call. I'll drive you to work."

As soon as Graham's car cleared the driveway, she turned her gaze on him. "How are things with you and Peter?"

Surprise showed clearly in his raised eyebrows and open mouth when he glanced at her. "You're asking me a personal question?"

She never asked personal questions. Lara was the queen of keeping things impersonal, yet she felt a little insulted by his reaction. "What? You know just because I don't always ask doesn't mean I don't care."

"Uh-huh," he glanced at her again, the gleam in his eyes speculative. "I think maybe dating Mr. Dawson has something to do with it."

"I'm not dating Karl. I'm fucking him."

"You've had dinner with him, he sent you flowers, and you went out with him again last night." Graham lifted a finger with each point until he was fluttering three of them in her face. "That's dating, sweetheart."

Shit. Panic fluttered in Lara's tummy but she squelched it, fast. "It's just sex, Graham. Your boss knows his way around a woman's body, and I'm enjoying it."

Graham sighed. "I know I wasn't exactly thrilled when you started dating him, but Lara, honey, the man is more than hot, he's a good guy. If you like him, I say go for it. It's about time a man gave you a run for your money."

She didn't need to ask what he meant by that. The way she could wrap men around her little finger was a running joke between them. Instead, she was curious . . . "Why the sudden change of heart?"

He gave her an arch look. "He sent you flowers that weren't a kiss-off bouquet."

Panic rose in Lara. "It was a thank-you. He thinks I'm good in bed, that's all. Don't read anything into it, Graham. It's just sex with us. Incredible sex," she muttered. "But still just sex."

"You keep saying that, maybe you'll convince yourself."

"How did we get on this topic anyway? I want to know what's up with you and Peter?"

Graham pulled into the parking lot of the warehouse and came to a stop at the staff entrance. When he faced her, his eyes were worried. "He's horny for a female, and I don't know what to do about it."

Okay, she'd asked. Now what was she supposed to do? Offer advice? A shoulder to cry on? He did look like he could burst into tears at any moment. Shit, what did she get herself into?

"Well, uhmm, I take it you don't want to uhmm, get him one?"

"No! What if he enjoys it so much he decides he's not gay anymore? I'd lose him!"

Lara's hand was on the doorknob, her muscles tense and ready to go. She hated to talk about emotions and stuff, but it was Graham, and despite herself, she cared for him.

Letting go of the door she turned in her seat to face him. "Graham, Peter loves you. He's let you into his home, and his heart, and letting him get naked with a woman isn't going to change that. Sex can just be sex, a physical urge, two bodies, two animals enjoying what comes naturally. It's not always making love. Do you trust him?"

Tears welled in his eyes and he nodded. "Yes. I mean, he could've just cheated, but he didn't. He told me what he wanted."

"See? There you go." She patted him on the shoulder. "He just needs a little pussy every now and then. It doesn't mean he won't always love you."

Graham leaned forward and wrapped his arms around her in a tight hug. "Thanks, Lara. You're a good friend."

Warmth flooded her and her lips split into a grin. She was a good friend.

Graham tensed and pulled back. "Uhmm, I think you're in trouble too."

Lara turned to see her boss standing at the staff entrance, arms folded across his barrel chest, eyebrows pulled into a bushy V.

Shit.

"Gotta go, Graham. Thanks for the ride."

She jumped out of the car and prepared for a bad day to get worse.

23

The incessantly ringing phone was getting on Karl's last nerve and he was ready to rip the phone lines right out of the wall when Graham finally sashayed in and parked his ass behind the reception desk.

Rising from his chair Karl strode out to the reception and glared down at his assistant. "You're late."

"Yes, I am. But I brought you coffee." Graham held out a cardboard cup. "Lara had some trouble this morning, and I had to drive her to work. There's a Starbucks right next to the warehouse she works out of and I couldn't resist."

Every muscle in Karl's body tensed. "Trouble? What kind of trouble?"

Graham waved around the cup he was still holding. "Don't you want the coffee?"

He took the cup and spoke through gritted teeth. "Thank you. Now tell me what kind of trouble Lara had."

"Someone slashed the tires on her car last night. Can you believe it? Peter thinks it was deliberate threat aimed at Lara too, since they left the knife stuck in the tire. Big knife."

Ice ran though Karl's veins, then fire. He dropped the file he was holding on Graham's desk and turned on his heel. "The papers are signed. File that and bill Ken Brand."

"Okeydokey."

He punched Lara's number into the phone and waited while the phone rang once, twice, the third ring cut off as Lara's harried voice answered. "Hey, Karl, how are you doing?"

"Not so well, sugar. Why did I have to hear it from Graham that someone has threatened you?"

"I wasn't threatened. Some punk just vandalized my car."

"Slashed tires is not vandalism, not if yours is the only car hit and they leave the knife. Graham's lover is right. That's a threat."

Her sigh echoed over the phone line. "I'm not going to argue about it, Karl. I'm having a shit day and it's not even noon yet."

"Lara." He stopped his pacing and softened his voice. She didn't need his fear or anger right now, she needed his strength. "Sugar, where are you right now?"

"Just getting ready to leave the lube shop on Hastings."

"Lube shop, hmm?"

That did the trick. His girl's dirty little mind immediately jumped on the innuendo and her chuckle soothed his nerves.

"That's my girl, I love to hear you laugh," he soothed. "You feel a little better?"

"Yes, thank you."

"Now tell me why you didn't call me this morning, so I could make you feel better then."

"Because it had nothing to do with you. What could you have done, Karl? It was probably just a case of mistaken identity anyway."

"I could've made you feel better, but that's not the point." He firmed his voice. "The point is that last night you agreed you were mine, and I take care of what's mine. I do not like hearing news second hand, and I especially do not like someone threatening what's mine."

"*I'm* not yours, Karl. My body is yours to use, I get that, and I even *like* that. But I'm still me, the same independent and bold woman you met almost two weeks ago. I've been taking care of myself for more than a decade and that's not going to change any time soon."

His muscles twitched as he put his head down and bit his tongue. Silence stretched between them and his temper faded, leaving him hurt and a little confused. How could she ignore the connection between them? It was so much more than physical.

Telling her that wouldn't be enough though. He was getting to know Lara better every minute. She was smart, but she was stubborn too. Telling her would accomplish nothing. He needed to show her. "Then you better bring your body to my office sometime this afternoon so I can make us both feel better."

"I'll try," she said.

"Don't try, sugar. Do it." He paused, listening to her breathing get heavier. "I have another call, so I have to go now. I'll see you when you get here."

He set the phone down and sank into his chair. She was fine, unhurt, and apparently as strong and brazen as ever. He, on the other hand, felt like he'd been sucker punched.

It didn't matter that it was only her car that was hurt, what mattered was that she hadn't trusted that he would be there for her. And no matter what she said, his gut was telling him that the threat had been directed at her. It wasn't a case of the wrong car, someone had done that to *her*.

She'd been in trouble, and she hadn't called him.

"I've been taking care of myself for more than a decade . . ."

She couldn't be more than twenty-five or twenty-six years old. That would mean she'd had to be strong when she was thirteen or fourteen. Sadness weighed down on his shoulders. He knew something had to have happened in her past to make her so tough, but for it to have happened when she was so young tore at his insides.

Those walls of cockiness and sexual confidence she'd built to hide behind were higher and stronger than he'd thought. The question was, were they too high?

They'd rushed things. *He'd* rushed things.

He'd let pure lust and Lara's obvious sexual eagerness distract him from the fact that she was completely untrained. Sure, Lara was naturally submissive. He could feel it. But she wasn't like any other submissive he'd met. She might think it was a game, but that was because to so many people, D/s *was* a game. Nothing more than a sexual kink to keep things interesting in the bedroom.

It was so much more than that though, and it was up to him to show her.

Karl had always known there was a deeper need inside himself. He enjoyed the play, and it kept the need from clawing up his insides, but that was only because he hadn't found the one that could feed his need. The one that could accept, and embrace, how deeply the need ran within him.

When he thought of Lara, when he looked at her, the urge to dominate, to own, to care for . . . and to love was stronger than anything he'd felt. And he sensed her need ran just as deep, she just hadn't accepted it yet.

Lara wasn't someone who would submit to a man just because he called himself a Dom. She'd only submit to someone who was strong enough to dominate her. He was that man. He wanted more than her body, and he was patient enough, and strong enough, to get it.

Then he'd always be her first call when something happened, and she'd trust enough to let him take care of her.

24

Lara worked through lunch to make up for being late, and she broke a few speeding laws to get her deliveries done with time to spare. She wondered at her eagerness to do what Karl had told her. Her first reaction had been to go about her day and deliberately be too busy to go see him. But as the day passed, and she wondered about what sort of fun he had in mind to make them both feel better, she started hurrying.

Normally if a guy told her to get her body somewhere by a certain time she'd tell him to get lost. Men were easy, and she really didn't need to put up with one who wanted to control her.

Yet, when Karl had given her that order, her breath had caught and desire had shot through her system. Desire that built up steam with every imagined scene of sitting on his desk and getting screwed hard and fast. And that was why she was eager.

It was natural. Karl Dawson was a prime male, with not only a big cock, but also the knowledge and imagination to use it well. In her almost twenty-seven years, she'd never met a man, or a woman, who could play her body the way he did.

Sure, it had been Jan's mouth that had given her the majority of her orgasms last night, but it had been at Karl's command. She couldn't wait to see what things his wicked imagination had come up with for their time in his office.

Graham's office day ended at five o'clock, so she figured Karl would be there at least until then. It being Wednesday, with not a lot of parts to be delivered, instead of pissing her boss off even more by going to see Karl when she had some slow time in the afternoon, she busted her butt to get her orders done by four. And she did it.

She dropped off the work truck and asked Maura to call her a cab.

Maura just looked at her and blew a smoke ring. "Where you going?"

She rattled off the address to Karl's office. "My friend works there. He'll give me a ride home."

"No need for a cab. John just made his last drop. I'll get him to deliver you as his last run." She winked and Lara chuckled.

As she walked away, she heard Maura get on the radio and tell the college student and part-time driver to pick her up in the parking lot. The April sun was shining. The streets sparkling from the light shower that had come out of nowhere an hour earlier, then disappeared five minutes after it had started. Typical Vancouver weather.

Why she was thinking about the weather she didn't know. Probably because she didn't want to think about her freakin' tires getting slashed, and she wasn't quite ready to examine her feelings for Karl.

Her feelings for Karl.

She'd known the man two weeks, he'd only fucked her once, and she had feelings for him. Something weird was happening, and she wasn't quite sure how she felt about it.

The little white delivery truck pulled into the parking lot and Lara jumped in. Fifteen minutes later she strode into Karl's building and noted that Graham was already gone. The door to Karl's office was open though. She stopped just inside it, drinking in the view of him at work.

Suit jacket off, sleeves rolled up to expose muscled forearms, and tie hanging loosely around his neck, he was pure masculine beauty. Not classically good-looking, or even handsome, but pure sensual delight. She breathed deep and imagined she could smell his earthy scent from where she stood. Her fingers itched to stroke through the mussed blond hair and down his neck, to the tense muscles of his shoulders.

"You look like you could use a massage," she said as she strolled into the room.

"Maybe I'll let you give me one." He lifted his head and gave her a small smile. "How was your afternoon?"

"Not bad."

He nodded. "Good. Go lock the front door, Lara, then come back and have a seat. I'll be done here in a minute."

She did as he told her, her blood heating and pulse jumping. He'd used *that tone*. The one that told her he was in Dom mode and made her mind start to fuzz over with lust.

After locking the door she perched herself in the visitor chair in front of his desk, hands in her lap and legs crossed at the ankles. A strange mixture of excitement and calm settled over her as she waited for him to finish his work.

He didn't make her wait long before he closed the file and set it aside. He stared at her, and she met his gaze. "Come here, Lara."

With no hesitation whatsoever she got up and walked to his side. He pushed his chair back and gestured for her to sit on his lap. She lifted a leg to straddle him but he shook his head. "No. Like this."

Large hands gripped her hips and pulled her down until she was sitting crosswise in his lap like a little girl on Santa's knee.

"I need to hold you," he said, pulling her head down until she was tucked against his chest. Citrusy cologne mixed with the musky scent of man blanketed her and she nuzzled her nose against the warm skin of his neck. One of his arm's snaked around her waist, and the other settled hotly on her thigh. "When I dropped you off at home last night, it was just after one in the morning, and I walked right past your car at the curb, twice, and there wasn't any damage."

"I tol—"

"I'm talking, Lara."

She snapped her mouth closed and snuggled against him

again. She hadn't even given her car a look when he'd dropped her off the night before. All of her focus had been on him, and her wonderfully exhausted body. Sort of like now. How did he expect her to listen when all she wanted to do was trace that tattoo with her tongue?

She parted her lips, and licked his neck. *Yum!* A warm hand stroked her hair, and she closed her eyes, a purr of contentment rumbling inside her. She opened her mouth and pressed it against his neck, laving it with her tongue, sucking gently as he talked.

"Do you know how it felt to hear from Graham that you were in trouble this morning? To know that you'd needed something, even if it was only a ride to work, and you didn't call me for it?"

She could hear the hurt in his voice, and her heart clenched. "My first instinct was to call you, but then I thought I was being silly."

"It's never silly to call me. Anytime, day or night, for anything, you call me. This thing between us is about more than sex, Lara. It's about us belonging to each other. About being able to give each other what we need. And I need you to trust that I will always be there for you, to give you what you need." He kissed the top of her head. "Even when it's not what you want."

That last part didn't sound so good.

Lara sighed. Emotions she didn't understand were swirling around in her stomach and she didn't know what to do. Her instinct was to cuddle closer to Karl and bask in being his, but her brain wouldn't let her. She'd learned the hard way that there was no one to depend on but herself and to believe otherwise was just asking for hurt.

But she wanted to. She really did want what he spoke of.

"Yes, Sir." She lifted her head and looked deep into his eyes.

He kissed her gently before lifting her off his lap. "Take your jeans off, sugar, and bend over the desk."

Heat flashed through her, spreading from her belly to the juncture of her thighs. Her nipples hardened instantly and began to ache for attention.

"Yes, Sir!" Pushing aside the confusing thoughts and emotions running through her, she unsnapped her jeans, kicked them off and stepped up to the desk.

She didn't need any foreplay. Her body was already trembling with the need to feel him deep inside her. She spread her legs and bent forward, bracing her hands on the hardwood desktop.

Karl leaned against her back, and spoke into her ear, his breath warm and moist on her skin. "You've joked about getting spanked a couple of times. Let's see how you like it, shall we?"

"Spanked?" She tried to straighten, but her back hit the solid wall of his chest. He had her pinned close to the desk; she couldn't straighten without asking him to move. And she wasn't about to do that.

"I want your body, your heart, and your soul, Lara. You said your body is mine, so I'm going to use it to get the rest. Starting with punishing you for worrying me."

His erection nudged against her ass and Lara repressed the shiver of anticipation than ran through her. An uncontrollable urge to push him, to explore what was happening took over her. "You've been looking for a reason to spank me since we met. Go ahead, I can take anything."

"You don't get it yet, do you, sugar?" He stepped back; one hand was left pressing into the middle of her back, forcing her down until her torso was stretched out along the top of the desk, the other hand stroked down her back and smoothed over her buttocks. "I don't need a reason to spank you. This body is mine, to do with what I please. If I want to spank—I spank."

His hand lifted and a loud smack echoed in the room as he brought his hand down sharply on her rounded cheek. Stinging pain shot through her, and she cried out.

"Hurts, does it?"

His words had barely faded when his hand came down again. "Holy shit!" *Why the hell had she agreed to try this submissive thing?*

"You can take it, sugar," he taunted. "My girl is tough." Smack!

"Independent." Smack!

"I'm sorry, Sir." The words jumped from Lara's lips in an effort to make him stop. Sure, she could just stand up and walk away. Karl didn't strike her as deranged or abusive, he wouldn't stop her. But that would mean quitting their game, and she wasn't ready to give up the pleasure he could dish out just because of a little pain.

"I know you're sorry, but that isn't enough." As he spoke, his hand rubbed over her heated cheeks, delivering small upward slaps to the under curve of her ass. "You need to understand and *accept* that just because your body enjoys this, it doesn't mean it's only sex."

Her mind rebelled, making her speak rashly. "I'm not enjoying this, Sir."

"Now, Lara, I explained to you, honesty and communication is key. Don't lie to me." Smack! Smack! Smack! Three blows in quick succession, the sound of his hard hand hitting her soft flesh blending with her cries in an erotic symphony.

Then he slid his hand over her throbbing cheeks and down between her thighs. "So hot, baby. You have to learn to trust me to know what you need. See how your body enjoys this? You've been asking for a spanking since we met. Twitching your tail and saying, 'Yes, Sir,' but holding part of yourself back from me and from yourself. See how much you like this, how wet you are, how much you needed this?"

His taunt hit home and silenced her. She bit down on her lip and pressed her hot forehead to the desktop, fighting the rioting sensations of her body. But he was right. Her mind might be rebelling at what he was doing, but her body loved it.

"You are a sexual submissive, sugar. You need this, your body craves it, and deep inside you know it. Don't be scared of your needs, they don't make you weak. They make you special." Her pussy lips thickened and the juices that had started flowing at the second smack of her ass were now coating her inner thighs. His voice was strong and deep, his words flowing into her ears and settling in her core.

He leaned forward, his fingers working her clit as his hard-on pressed against her hip and his chest rubbed against the side of her body. His breath tickled her ear as he spoke, softly this time. "We're in this together, you and I. All the way." Warm lips pressed against the soft spot beneath her ear, soothing her.

A shudder ripped through her. *All the way?*

He stood and removed his fingers from her clit, rubbing his hand over her ass again. "You already gave me your body. This is mine, right?"

She nodded, a unique calmness settling over her. Her mind starting to float along the sensations he'd created in her body.

"My body to protect." Smack!

"My body to punish." Smack!

"My body to pleasure." Smack!

Tears streamed silently down Lara's cheeks, as she lay bent over the desk in submission. The pain had crossed a line into pleasure and intense satisfaction, narrowing her world to only this moment. To his voice, his hand, and the heat and hunger of her empty pussy. She unconsciously spread her thighs farther apart, opening herself up to him, for whatever he wanted to do to her.

"No more hiding behind your lusts, your wants," he said as he stepped behind her.

The rasp of his zipper going down started a trembling deep within her. *Oh, yes!*

He kicked her feet farther apart, and the head of his cock nudged against her sex. "But I know you," he crooned. "I see beyond my girl's wants, to her needs. And you need this, don't you? You need me inside you."

"Oh, yes!" The calmness she'd felt was fading, swallowed up by the overwhelming hunger to take him inside her. She wanted that cock so bad. She'd wanted it since the first second she met him, and every minute since. "Fuck me, Karl. Please."

With one smooth thrust, he filled her. Strong hands gripped her waist and he pumped hard and fast into her, his balls bouncing against her clit as his belly slapped against her burning ass cheeks. Her fingers curled around the edge of the desk and she closed her eyes, reveling in the feel of him.

"Thank you. Thank you, Sir. Yes, yes, I needed this." Her cunt instantly tightened around his cock in spasms of pleasure as her body rejoiced in the pleasure of being used. "Can I come? Sir, can I come?"

"God you feel good. So hot and tight and wet. Your cunt sucks at me with every move. Feel that? Feel how good we fit?" Karl's voice became ragged as he spoke, his hips pumping faster, harder.

Her insides tightened, everything tightened. He kept slamming into her, his cock hitting deep with every thrust as she panted and cried and begged. She was going to come! She couldn't come, he hadn't said she could come! "Karl! Please! Can I come?"

"Yes!" He roared his answer, his fingers digging into her hips as he bent his knees and lodged himself so deep inside that her feet lifted off the ground. Hot liquid shot from his body to hers as his cock swelled and jerked inside her spasming core.

When she could breathe again, the first thing she did was speak. "Thank you."

Karl's heart skipped a beat at her soft words and he slipped his hands beneath her. Lifting, he stepped back, carrying her with him as he found his chair.

Once again, he arranged her in his lap. He put a shaking finger under her chin and lifted her face to his.

"What's between us is more than sex, Lara. *That* was more than sex." He kissed the streaks left on her cheeks from her dried tears, his chest tightening at the salty taste.

Fear clouded her eyes, and he sensed panic trying to get ahold of her. He stroked a gentle hand up and down her back, his gaze never leaving hers as he strove to keep her calm.

"Shhhhh, it's okay," he murmured. "I was wrong to withhold myself from you last night. You needed me too much, and it's too soon for you to truly trust that I'll always give you what you need, even if it's not right away. But I can only do that if you're honest with me and with yourself, Lara."

He kissed her then, his tongue gently coaxing hers into play. Her arms crept up and around his neck, and she melted into him, giving him the comfort they both needed.

25

She sat on Karl's lap, kissing and cuddling and soaking up his warmth. Eyes closed, cradled against him, she was surrounded, safely cocooned in his energy. She got it, now. The burning of her freshly spanked ass was a badge of her strength, and his concern.

After a short while, Karl patted her hip and told her to get dressed, he was going to take her home. She floated through getting dressed and the drive home as if in a dream, her head full but unwilling to delve too deeply into her thoughts just then.

Instead, she focused on Karl's constant touching. His hand at her back, keeping his hand on top of hers when she placed it on his thigh, holding her hand as he walked her to the door. It felt so good when she was with him. Better than good, she felt sexy and beautiful and safe and cared for.

She felt cherished.

It was weird, but being with him excited her, and at the same time, calmed something deep within. Something she hadn't even been aware of before.

She unlocked her door and turned to him. "Will you come in? I'll cook you dinner." The words were out of her mouth before she knew what she was saying. They certainly weren't what she'd planned, but the thought of him leaving just then was too much for her. She wasn't ready to say good-bye.

His eyes lit up and his smile set the butterflies to fluttering in her stomach. "I'd like that. Thanks, sugar."

He came in and sat at the kitchen table while she searched the cupboards for ideas. She wasn't a gourmet or anything, but she enjoyed cooking, and she really wanted to make something nice for Karl.

"Water, Coke, or coffee?" she asked when she opened the fridge.

"Real Coke, or diet?"

"Definitely real. Real stuff always has the best flavor. Like butter." She held up the container she'd just pulled from the fridge. "No man-made margarine here. Real butter is better."

That set the tone, and Lara was pleased that Karl kept things light. They made small talk while she wrapped some salmon in tinfoil with butter and herbs and then slid them into the oven. By the time she was slicing and dicing fresh veggies, they were laughing over the story of his first fishing trip with his dad.

"I loved the camping, loved the fire, and the tent, but something about being in a small canoe out on the Pacific Ocean, even though we weren't way out there, just made my balls shrivel up and hide."

Lara loved that he'd admit to a fear. "So are you still scared of the water?"

"Not if I'm on a big boat or a ferry."

Her heart skipped a beat at his self-deprecating smile. "It sounds like you had a good childhood."

"I did. My parents had a good marriage, and they loved me." He nodded, his gaze steady on her. "I was lucky, not everyone has that as an example of how things can be."

She opened the fridge, searching for something, anything, to do so that she didn't have to meet his gaze. She didn't want to talk about families and childhoods. She'd worked too hard to put hers behind her.

"I don't have anything for dessert. I wasn't planning on cooking for company."

Karl grabbed her hand and pulled her over to stand between his knees. He kissed her knuckles, his tongue skimming the sensitive skin between her fingers. "I think we had dessert before we left the office."

The purr in his voice reached deep inside her and stroked her sex. Locking her knees to stop the trembling that had started there, she licked her lips, trying to think of something to say, anything to say.

"You weren't one of the lucky ones, were you?" he asked softly.

She shook her head, avoiding his gaze, but unable to ignore the question. "It wasn't perfect, but it could've been worse."

"Want to tell me about it?" His thumb caressed the palm of her hand, giving her a solid connection to something warm. Giving her strength.

She met his gaze, a small smile lifting her lips as she shrugged. "There's nothing to tell. My mom left when I was little, and my dad was a drunk who couldn't keep a job."

"So you not only had to take care of yourself, but of him too." Karl's body remained relaxed, slouched in the chair with her standing between his knees, but she could sense the tension grow in him, see the anger in his eyes. Not anger at her, but *for her.*

"For a while—then I left. It's easier to look after myself when I'm the only person I need to worry about."

"I know you've been looking after yourself for a long time. More than a decade you said, but I meant what I said—what we have is special. We're in this together, Lara, all the way. You just have to decide if you're brave enough to give it a chance."

She just stood there, heart thumping against her ribs, brain completely frozen, drowning in the dark pools of his eyes until the timer on the oven started screaming.

She dashed for the oven, snatching up the dish towel as she went. Karl's last statement was a testament to not only what he wanted, but also just how well he did know her. It had been a direct challenge, and she never turned her back on a challenge.

As if she'd been jolted out of a trance, her mind raced as she got their plates ready. Everything he'd said in his office came back full force. *His* . . . he wanted her. He really wanted *her*—not just her body. Part of her knew he was right. There was more than just sex to them. No one had ever made her feel the way he did. No one had ever gotten her so wrapped up in *feeling* and *sensation* that she'd say anything, do anything, forget everything but his touch and his voice.

No one had ever made her feel as cared for, or as safe as he did, either. When she was in his arms, she felt . . .

Lara gave her head a shake. She didn't know what she felt, but she did know she needed to think before accepting that challenge, no matter how strongly the desire to just say *"Let's do it"* was.

Loading the plates full of veggies, rice, and fish, she watched out of the corner of her eye as Karl opened the laptop she'd left on the table, and hit a few keys. Nickleback filled the small space just as she set the plates on the table.

"A little mood music to go with the meal," he said with a grin.

She shot him a look. "Yeah, funny how the first words of that song are 'I like your pants around your feet.' "

"It seems appropriate."

They laughed and the light mood was restored.

It was unusual how comfortable she was having him in her house. The boys came down to watch movies every now and then, but it was their house too. She'd had men over before but they only ever saw her bedroom, and maybe the shower if they were lucky.

Cooking for someone, just chatting and enjoying each other's company, was something totally new for her. And she liked it.

She liked Karl.

It went beyond the banked heat that was in his eyes and the sparks that went through her every time their fingers brushed or their knees bumped. The pleasure she got when he bit into his salmon and moaned appreciatively was matched only by the joy of verbally sparring with him.

He was quick and funny, and she loved that even though he'd been spanking her ass an hour ago, he didn't feel the need to try and constantly dominate her.

As if the natural conversation didn't prove that, when dinner was done and she stood to clear the plates, he helped.

"You wash, I'll dry," he said, grabbing a dish towel and standing at her side.

"I'm surprised you don't want to wash since you like to dip your fingers into the wetness so much."

"It's the bubbles." He looked at her, completely straight-faced. "I prefer smooth and creamy wetness."

She snorted. "No doubt!"

He laughed and they made quick work of the dishes. When she bent over to put away the cutting board, she felt the light snap of a towel against her ass.

"Hey!" She straightened up covering her backside with her hands. "My butt is sensitive enough right now, thank you very much."

He tried to look shamed, but the grin kept him from pulling it off. "I couldn't resist when you bent over like that."

"Oh yeah?" She snatched up the other tea towel and started to twirl it menacingly. "Prepare for battle, buddy."

She took a fighting stance and flicked her wrist, snapping the towel at his thigh. Quicker than she could blink he grabbed the towel and tugged her against his chest. "I'd rather just say thank you for a wonderful dinner," he said before his mouth slanted over hers.

Lara opened for him without hesitation. She dropped the towel and wrapped her arms around his neck, her tongue meeting his, dancing and rubbing as she leaned into him.

He pulled back and nipped at her bottom lip, a growl rumbling from his chest and fluttering over her. "I need to get going."

A sigh rose within her, but she squelched it. What was her problem? She'd been with him for hours the night before, and again for hours that evening. She should be sick of him, she should be craving her own space, not wanting to hang on to him.

"Yeah, it's getting late and I need to go talk to Peter about my car." She pulled her arms back and tried to take a step back only to have his hands grip her hips and hold her in place. He tapped his forehead lightly against hers, and she gazed up at him.

"We're not going to see each other again until next week, sugar. I need you to think about what we've done, and all I've said. I am a Dom, and I need a sub. I think that's you, but only you can decide for sure." His hand slid around and squeezed her tender butt cheeks. "We will stay in touch though. You have my email, and my phone numbers; you can call me *anytime*, for any reason. Understood?"

Lara nodded, her chest tight.

Her first instinct was to ask why she couldn't see him for so long, but she bit her tongue. She did need to think. So, she forced a confident smile, and spoke firmly. "Understood."

"Okay then." He pressed a quick hard kiss to her lips and stepped back. "Thank you for a wonderful dinner. It was just what I needed."

"You're welcome." She walked him to the door, giving him a cheerful wave before closing the door on his retreating form and leaning against it.

After a minute of looking at her empty suite, listening to the tinny notes of music still coming from her laptop, she spun on her heel and headed for the stairway to Peter and Graham's floor.

She did have to say thank you to Peter for dealing with her car issues, she did *not* suddenly feel a little lost.

26

Lara couldn't sleep. Again.

Every time she closed her eyes, Karl appeared to her, dressed in his leather pants with his wicked tattoo and light glinting off the jewelry in his nipples. In her mind he was standing there, arms wide open, saying "You can have me . . . if you dare."

If she dared.

After living on the streets as a runaway for three of her teenage years, she dared pretty much anything. Except letting people get too close. She'd learned the hard way, her first year on the streets, that letting people too close was a good way to get hurt. Emotions hurt.

Emotions other than pleasure that is.

Lara knew that's why she loved sex so much; it was the only time she really let herself go, the only time she really let herself feel. It was a safe outlet for her because she only took lovers who would want no-strings sex.

Karl was supposed to be that way. Graham thought his lectures about Karl going through women or not wanting a girlfriend would stop her, but really, it had only encouraged her. And she was thankful, because the sex with Karl *was* good.

Hell, it was better than any she'd ever had.

Now it was more than that. She actually enjoyed spending time with him. Talking to him, joking with him . . . being with him. When was the last time she'd enjoyed another person's company so much? Not just a man, but anyone?

It's what happened after the sex that really got to her. He was strong and dominant, and yet, oh so gentle and caring. She didn't have any defenses against that gentleness. It crawled into her system, and made her want more.

She didn't even know what more was! She knew nothing about relationships—she hadn't even had a relationship with her own parents.

"For fuck sake," the little voice in her head said. *"Just ask him. He wanted you to think about it . . . so ask him!"*

So out of bed she went. She grabbed her iBook off the kitchen table and hustled back to bed. It was late, and he wouldn't get the email until morning at the earliest, but she had to get her thoughts out, or she'd never get any rest.

Good Morning, Karl.

I've been lying in my bed tossing and turning, trying to fall asleep, but I can't. I can't sleep because I can't stop thinking about you and the things you said tonight.

You said we'd keep in touch this week and I should take some time to think about it all, but I need answers now. You've also always said I could ask you anything.

So, here goes anything.

Just what exactly do you want from me? I've been on my own for a long time, and I like it that way. I like my space and my independence. I'm not going to try and deny that I also like what you do to my body, but I also have to admit that the intensity of this . . . thing between us sort of freaks me out a bit.

You're right though. It's not just the sex. It's everything you make me feel, so my question is . . . if I decide that maybe I do want to work on this, that maybe taking it beyond strictly sexual is something I want to try, how do we do that?

I know you're going to say "Trust You". Isn't that what all submissives are supposed to do . . . trust their Dom? But it's not as easy as that. Not for me. I need to know what you have in mind. This is all new to me—not just the Dominant/submissive thing, but any sort of a relationship that is beyond casual.

So, now that I've made a complete idiot of myself by admitting I'm almost twenty-seven years old and never had a real relationship of any kind . . . I'm going to say good night and hit send before I chicken out.

Lara

She closed her eyes, hit send, and then clapped her hands over her face. "Oh God, what am I getting myself into?"

Sucking in a deep breath, she blew it out slowly, and her pounding heart calmed. Before panic could get ahold of her, she closed her computer down and shut out the light.

It was done.

Sure it was easier to spill her guts in an email than in person, but now she had to wait for a reply.

Waiting was not one of her strong suits.

27

I don't know why you keep that crappy job anyway," Graham said as he set the steaming teapot in the middle of their table.

Lara heaved a sigh and reached out to pour herself another cup. "It's a good job, regular hours, regular paycheck. Security is important to me."

She'd woken up early, unable to sleep, and had heard his footsteps above her head. Figuring misery loved company, she went upstairs for breakfast before work. Breakfast being tea and toast.

"Yes," Graham said with a smirk. "But your paycheck isn't exactly big. You can't even live on what you make, let alone pay a three hundred dollar ticket, and you work thirty-five hours a week!"

"I've got the money, it just sucks completely because I *did* stop. That bitch needs glasses." She'd just finished telling him about how she'd gotten pulled over by a lady cop the day before . . . for rolling through a red light on a right turn.

"Of course, I wasn't stupid enough to say that to her," she grimaced at Peter.

"Smart." He nodded his approval.

"The point isn't that you got a ticket, or even that the company won't cover it," Graham continued. "The point is that you have a ticket to pay. What right does the company have to fine you? In fact, I should ask Mr. Dawson. I bet it's illegal for them to fine you for getting a ticket."

Her eyebrows snapped down so fast she gave herself a headache. "Don't. You. Dare."

"What? He *is* a lawyer, you know?"

"Try the innocent look on someone who doesn't know you, Graham. My getting a speeding ticket is none of Karl's business. I'm still pissed at you for telling him about the tires. If you ever want me to speak to you again, you'll keep your mouth zipped."

Graham arched a brow at Peter. "She's pretty adamant, isn't she?"

"Very. I wonder why?"

Maybe because two days later my ass is still tender? "Because things with Karl are complicated right now, that's all."

"Ohhh. Details, details, please." Graham rubbed his hands together.

"Graham," Peter growled. "Take it easy on her."

Graham stared at Peter and the temperature in the kitchen dropped a few degrees. "Why?"

"It's okay, Peter," she said before the two could get into an argument. "It's not a big deal. Things are just moving fast, and maybe getting more serious than I want. It's not a big deal."

But Graham had heard the one word she should've left out. "*Maybe* getting more serious than you want? What's with the maybe, sweetheart? You've always been the ultimate Alpha Loner Chick, is that changing? Have you *maybe* met your Alpha Man?"

She rolled her eyes and tried to shrug him off. "Don't be so dramatic. We like each other, we have good chemistry, and who knows . . . maybe it's time I gave having a steady man in my life a try."

The complete silence in the room was unnerving. Lara licked her thumb and used it to pick up the crumbs from her toast that had fallen on the table.

"I think that's great, Lara. You deserve to have someone who'll look after you." Graham smiled softly and she relaxed.

That sounded good. She didn't even feel the need to state that she didn't need someone to look after her.

A nd you said he wouldn't pay."

Karl could swear he saw a canary feather flutter to the floor from Lisa Pollock's lips. The woman definitely had the look of a cat with a full belly.

They'd had an early negotiation meeting with Brad Pollock and his lawyer, and while his client had what she wanted, he couldn't shake the ugly feeling in the pit of his stomach.

"I'm glad you're happy, Lisa," he said as he opened her car door for her. "Will you tell me how you got those photos now?"

"Why are you so interested in that?" she asked.

He forced a smile. "I need good investigators myself sometimes. To get photos like that, yours must be very good."

She nodded, her gaze unreadable behind her sunglasses. "I'll call you with the name when Brad's first check shows up."

She got into the car and he closed the door behind her, waving her off. It wasn't his responsibility to find out who took the pictures, but he couldn't help but try. No one deserved to be photographed in a vulnerable position, in a place where they'd been assured safety and anonymity. He'd do what he could, but he had no doubt Mason Hardin would get to the bottom of it no matter what. That man's polished exterior definitely hid something dangerous.

Karl went back into the parking garage and climbed into his truck. The trip back to his office was quick, and Karl's mind was four steps ahead of him the minute he stepped into his office.

He pulled a folder from his briefcase and handed it to Graham. "Get those filed as quick as possible, and close out Lisa Pollock's account. When's my next appointment?"

"Fifteen minutes," Graham traded files with him. "Janet Redding, a potential new client."

"Another woman," he muttered. "Why do I only get the female clients?"

Graham sat back in his chair and ran his eyes up and down Karl's body in an exaggerated perusal. "Gee, I don't know, Mr. Dawson."

"Stop eating me up with your eyes or I'm telling your boyfriend," Karl smirked and headed for his office. "And stop staring at my ass."

It was unprofessional of him to say something like that to his assistant, but the way Graham's jaw had dropped had been worth it. Besides, he was a friend of Lara's, so there was some leeway.

He tossed his briefcase down, booted up his computer, and headed for the coffee pot. Coffee, he needed coffee. He'd been in a rush that morning, distracted by thoughts of how he could've been waking up with Lara, and hadn't had any coffee yet.

It was much needed to keep his head from exploding.

He poured a cup, took a scalding swallow, and opened his email program. Lara's name was at the top of the inbox, and he froze. Was she backing out already? The way his morning had gone, his sassy sub would probably try to run.

Setting his coffee down he clicked on her name and started reading. His mouth went dry and his palms started to sweat. She wasn't running. She wasn't jumping in with both feet . . . but she wasn't running!

He read the email and then reread it. Then reread it again, with so many possible responses at the tip of his fingertips when he hit reply. He wanted to answer everything, he wanted to answer the question she hadn't asked yet, but he knew would follow. He couldn't scare her away though. She was right on the edge and he had to be careful. He did not want to fuck it up.

With a deep breath, he started typing.

Of course you can always ask me anything. And if you need answers now, I'll give them to you.

Let's start with what I want from you. What I want is just what I said. I want you to realize that what we have is more than sex. I want you to accept it and work with me toward building this into a real relationship.

You're very brave to tell me that you're a little freaked out, and I appreciate it. To know how you are feeling, what you are thinking, is what I need. Now I want you to realize something . . . you are already giving this a chance, simply by asking these questions and talking to me.

Welcome to our relationship, Lara.

28

Lara's first urge when she got home from work on Thursday was to open up her computer and see if Karl had answered her email. But her brain wouldn't let her. Instead she headed upstairs to chat with Peter before Graham got home, but she took her phone with her, just in case he called instead of emailing.

"Knock knock," she called out when she didn't see Peter in the kitchen or living room. "Is it a bad time?"

"Perfect timing, actually." Peter came out of the second bedroom, his "office," scrubbing his fingers through his hair. "If I don't get away from the computer, I'm going to put my fist through the screen any minute now."

"Writer's block?"

He shook his head. "Stubborn characters. I need a drink."

He grabbed a couple of beers from the fridge and they sat at the kitchen table. "What's up, Lara?"

She took her time getting comfortable, twisting off the beer bottle cap, and putting her feet up on the chair across from her. "What makes you think something's up? I can't just come say hi?"

He stared at her.

"Fine. I want to see how you and Graham are doing."

Peter cocked his head to the side, his eyes laughing. "We're doing fine. How are you and Karl?"

She grimaced. Her and Karl. Like they were already a couple in people's minds. "That's not fair. You and Graham have been together since I've known you. I care if you guys are having trouble."

"I care if you're having trouble with Karl."

Was she having trouble with Karl? Or was she just having trouble with the idea of anyone getting close? Shit, that sort of self-analysis was what she was trying to avoid at the moment.

"We can talk about me later. Spill. Graham's pretty worried about you craving a woman, you know?"

Peter choked on his beer, a bit of the foamy liquid spewing onto the table. She got up and grabbed the paper towel while he tried to get his breath back. "He told you that?"

"Yes."

He took the towel from her and wiped the table, and the front of his shirt. Then his mouth as he looked at her. "Did he mention who it was I've been . . . desiring?"

"No." She tried to hide her surprise. "I didn't know it was someone specific, I thought it was just a woman. You know, craving a little pussy."

"I'm surprised he said anything to you at all. When did you guys talk about this?"

"When he drove me to work after my tires were messed up."

Peter's frown deepened. "About that." He fiddled with the label on his beer bottle. "Did he find your tires like that, or did you?"

Lara's shoulders tensed. "I did. Why?"

Peter took another long swallow from his beer then met her gaze. "Because it's not just any woman I've been fantasizing about. It's you, and Graham knows it."

"Huh?" Her mind went blank. Her?

They'd flirted, and she did think Peter was kind of hot, but she'd never really thought about joining them. Watching them together, yes. But not being with one of them.

Wait a minute!

She held up a hand for silence while she picked her jaw up off the floor. When she could, she spoke slowly, clearly. "You asked me if it was me who found my tires slashed or him. Does that mean you think *he* might've done it?"

Peter scrubbed a hand over his face. "No. I don't think so. I don't know. He's hurt and angry, and he likes to throw his little tantrums sometimes, so yes, the thought crossed my mind."

Lara shook her head. "No way. I don't believe he'd be capable of that. I can't believe you think he is!"

"I can't believe it, either." Lara's head swiveled and she spotted Graham just inside the door, staring at Peter.

Karl slouched on the bar stool, beer in hand, and watched his friend count beer and weigh liquor bottles in preparation for the bar's opening.

The workday had finished without Lara responding to his latest email and that stressed him a bit. He wanted to call her, but he really had no clue how to go about dealing with her. He was used to play partners and dates, not starting a relationship. Especially one with a woman who was also pretty inexperienced in that department.

"I have a little problem," Karl finally said.

Val didn't miss a beat. "I figured."

"I think I'm in love."

"The woman with the emails?" He put the Bailey's bottle on the back bar and grabbed the Kahlua one. When it was on the scale and measured, he moved on to the Grand Marnier, not even looking up at Karl.

"One and the same."

Val glanced at him. "I knew there was something special about her. So what's the problem?"

"She doesn't feel the same."

That made Val stop what he was doing and stare. Heat started to creep up Karl's neck and he avoided his friend's gaze, until finally he couldn't stand the silence anymore.

He gave Val a look. "What?"

"I'm in shock."

"Well get over it, man. I need help here."

"Now, now boys, play nicely." Samair stepped behind the bar and rubbed a hand over Val's back while she smiled at Karl. "What's new, Karl?"

Val answered before he could. "He's in love."

Great. "Tell the whole world why don't you?" He glared.

Samair's smile turned slightly evil. "It's about time."

"I said I *think* I'm in love." He gave backtracking a try. "For all I know it's just a stress headache coming on."

He was lying and they all knew it. He'd never even hint at being in love unless he was one hundred percent certain.

"When do we get to meet her?" Samair asked.

"There's a little problem. Apparently she doesn't feel the same way about him."

"Really?" Samair didn't bother to hide her glee. She grinned at Val, and then turned to Karl, blond eyebrow arched and a devil in her eye. "So you've finally met a woman who won't get on her knees and say, 'Yes, Master,' to your every command?"

Lara had no problem getting on her knees for him, but he wasn't going to tell them that. Hell, he didn't even know why he said anything.

Then he saw the way Samair shifted closer to Val, her hip bumping his until Val's arm went around her waist. That was why he said something. They were a couple that had gone through the whole damn song and dance of "It's just sex" before they finally admitted their feelings. They had knowledge he needed. So he needed to be honest.

"Lara has no problem getting on her knees for me, or any other position. I'm pretty sure she'd even call me Master if that was what I wanted," he looked Samair in the eye, "which it isn't."

"Then what do you want?"

What did he want? Lara had asked him, and his first instinct was to say, "Everything." But was it really possible to have everything?

He looked at Val and Samair. A couple that had started out as a "just sex" or "just entertainment" couple. They had it all. They were in love, they lived together, and they even worked out of the same building, Val having leased his extra storage room to Samair for her design office. They had it all.

"I want it all."

Samair leaned forward and put her hand over his. "Then tell her. Make it clear what you want, and don't let her get away."

He looked into her eyes and hope stirred in him. Could it be that simple? If he just spelled it all out for her, in his own way—since some of what he wanted was a bit out of the norm—would he get it?

He stood up and nodded to his friends. One thing was clear . . . if he didn't go for it, he'd for sure never get it.

29

The bottom dropped out of Peter's stomach at the sound of Graham's voice. Damn it! How come he hadn't heard the door open? He'd been too damn focused on Lara, that was why.

"I think it's time for me to leave," she said, rising from her chair.

"No, you stay." Graham's hand came down on her shoulder, his fiery gaze pinning Peter to his own seat. "Obviously it's me who isn't wanted here."

"Don't be silly, Graham. You know damn well I don't want you to leave. And Lara's right, I think this is between us."

"Oh, no!" Graham waved his finger in the air. "Not if you think my not wanting to share you with her, or any other woman, would drive me to violent vandalism. Is that why you said the knife still being there was a threat? Did you really think I was threatening Lara to stay away from you?"

"No! Yes, no. I don't know, Graham." Peter's palms began to sweat and his head hurt. "I'm sorry. I didn't want to think so, but it happened right after we had that fight, and my mind . . ." He let his words trail off. He had no words to explain. He'd fucked up and he knew it.

As Graham stood there, looking down at Peter, he could literally see the anger drained from Graham. His shoulders slumped, his eyes teared up, and his bottom lip began to quiver.

"How could you possibly think I was capable of something like that, Peter? You're supposed to know me, to *love* me."

Heart pounding and blood pumping Peter shot out of his chair and rushed to stand in front of Graham. He grabbed Graham by the arms and gave him a small shake. "I do love you! Don't ever doubt that!"

"How can you love me and think I'd ever want to hurt Lara?"

Graham tried to shake off Peter's hand, but Peter would not let go. He was never going to let go. His heart cracked and pain filled his chest. He had so not meant to hurt Graham. Graham was his boy, his love. "I'm sorry, baby. I've just been so wrapped up in this thriller and my characters are messing with my head. I think I was seeing crime and menace everywhere."

Graham sniffled and made another half-hearted attempt at getting away from him.

"I guess I'm just a bit messed up with the way things have been lately. You've been so cold and distant," Peter admitted softly.

Graham's eyes grew wide. "What do you expect when you tell me you're lusting after Lara and I'm right here?"

"I'd never want Lara more than you, Graham. And I'd never want to lose you over any woman!" He grabbed Graham by the back of the neck and kissed him long and hard. He put everything he had into that kiss, all of his love and loneliness, his passion and his hunger for his boy. It was home.

"Uhmm, I'm still here, guys," Lara's voice intruded. "I'd leave, but you're blocking me in."

Peter pulled back from the kiss and shifted Graham so he was leaning against the kitchen counter. "Don't move," he whispered before turning back to Lara.

"I'm sorry about this," he said.

Lara stood and raised her hand. "Don't be sorry. I didn't mean to start anything or get in the way at all. I'll just head back down to my place."

"Okay, but before you go I need you both to know something." He did want Lara, and they all knew it, but there was something else that he needed everyone to understand. "Yes, I find you attractive, and I'd very much enjoy fucking you. I know we'd both enjoy it. But I love Graham, heart and soul, and I'll never jeopardize that, and I'll never doubt him again."

Lara looked at him, her smile almost wistful. "That's good, Peter. You know I'm always up for flirting with you—with *both* of you." She glanced over his shoulder at Graham. "But that's all it is."

Peter met her gaze. "We're good?"

She leaned in and gave him a quick kiss. "We're good."

Peter didn't bother to watch her walk away. Instead, he turned to his boy. He had a point to make.

Once downstairs Lara realized she forgot her cell phone on the kitchen table and started back up to get it, but when she reached for the doorknob, telltale groans and whispers stilled her hand. Unable to stop herself, she gently turned the handle and peeked in.

Her breath caught in her throat. Peter was on his knees in front of Graham, his mouth full of cock.

Goosebumps rose on Lara's skin and she bit her lip. She shouldn't watch. She really shouldn't . . . but she couldn't take her eyes off them. It had always been obvious that Peter was the dominant one of the pair, so seeing him on his knees, loving Graham so thoroughly, was both touching and so very hot.

She tore her gaze from Peter's mouth and watched Graham's tense face as he worked to prevent himself from coming. His hands were braced on the kitchen counter and his eyes were glued to what Peter was doing to him.

"Enough," he begged. "Get up, please."

Peter pulled his mouth away, saliva dripping on his chin as he gazed up at Graham. "I'm yours, just as much as you are mine, baby. I need you to know that. To believe it."

"I do believe it. But I need you the way I love you. I've never wanted you on your knees for me, Peter. I need you on top, I need you in me."

Her eyes widened as what Graham said hit home. She'd said almost the same thing to Karl. She'd certainly thought it, felt it. Hearing someone else echo her thoughts, made them feel less scary. Her neediness, her hunger for Karl wasn't so unusual.

Lara watched as Peter got up off his knees and kissed Graham. His hands framed Graham's head, and she saw mouths open, tongues rub. She licked her lips. God, it was hot! Who knew watching two men would be so hot? But really, it didn't matter that it was two men. It was the feeling, the emotion that was so thick in the air.

Peter's hands shifted from Graham's head to his hips, and he suddenly spun him around.

"Get rid of the pants and bend over," he commanded. "Spread your cheeks and show me the way home, my boy." Peter reached for the bottle of olive oil that was next to the stove and unscrewed the cap. He made quick work of his own zipper and generously coated his prominent cock.

He dribbled a bit of oil over the puckered hole displayed for him, and rubbed it in with a gentle fingertip. Graham moaned, and Peter took up a solid stance.

She watched Peter grip his hard cock and inch closer to the hole in front of him as her own hand skimmed across sensitive nipples, pinching them through her shirt.

Another moan echoed through the kitchen, this time louder and clearer, as Peter slowly fed his cock into the well-slicked hole. The moan was cut off as Graham bit his lip and his head dropped forward onto the countertop.

Lust kept Lara's feet rooted to the floor, one hand teasing her nipples as the other rubbed the seam of her jeans over her clit. She wanted to undo her pants and reach in, but too much movement would draw the boys' attention, and then the action would stop . . . and she was enjoying the show way too much.

She desperately wanted to either leave, or join in, but her feet wouldn't move in either direction.

Her gaze was glued to Peter's ass as he thrust fast and hard into Graham. He hadn't come yet and the effort it took showed in his tense muscles. She watched as he reached around to grip Graham's erection and give it a few tugs. Her mouth watered. For a split second, she wanted to be on the floor between Graham's legs, sucking on his cock while Peter fucked him.

She closed her eyes, savoring the image as the sounds of skin slapping skin and male grunts and groans filled her head. A loud groan sounded and Lara opened her eyes in time to see Graham's cock jerk and twitch as white come shot from the tip and hit the counter. Peter's eyes slid shut and his buttocks clenched on one last thrust. His mouth opened and a victorious shout filled the room.

Then he collapsed forward, his chest covering Graham's back, his arms going around them. Lara saw his lips moving, but he couldn't hear the murmured words. Suddenly she felt that she was intruding.

Quiet as she could, she pulled the door closed and tiptoed down the stairs. Again, it wasn't the sex that had seemed so intimate to her, but the closeness the boys shared afterward.

Her knees weakened and she sat down on the bottom step—hard.

If she couldn't handle even watching the two of them be so open and loving, so intimate—how the hell was she ever going to have a real relationship with Karl?

30

All day long Friday Karl waited for a response from Lara and got nothing.

As he drove home, he couldn't stop himself from driving by her house. Her car was there, but he didn't stop to go inside. *Create the need, then fill it.* The way to train a submissive.

He was creating her need for him by staying away. He would fill it, as soon as she acknowledged it. What shocked him was how being away from her was creating such a strong need in himself.

He knew himself pretty well. A person had to when they played in the BDSM world the way he did. And that was the biggest truth he'd learned in the last couple of days of soul searching. He would happily give up playing in The Dungeon for her.

He was a Dom, and he would always be a Dom, but he didn't need the polyamorous lifestyle. He didn't need multiple play-mates, he didn't need the title of Sir or Master. It did send a thrill through him every time Lara called him Sir, more so than any other sub, but it was because he'd told her right from the start that she didn't have to.

Which meant when she did it, it was natural.

Just like her submitting to him was natural.

Them, together, was natural.

So why the hell hadn't she responded to his email?

Simone had said he'd just been skimming the surface with his play, and she was right. He knew the physical techniques of what he was doing, he knew the protocols and the etiquettes. But that stuff didn't matter when it came to Lara.

She wasn't from the scene, she wasn't a trained submissive, or even someone who came to him already well aware of her desire to submit. And the more he thought about it, he was glad of that. He liked that her submission was all-natural and that he was the only one who had ever aroused it in her. It stirred a primitive need in him that only her willingness could fill.

He pulled into the driveway of the nice old bungalow-style house he called home. It was the one his parents had bought and lived in their whole lives—He'd live in it his whole life, no matter how much money he made.

He'd renovated it a bit, upgraded some things and sound-proofed it better, but it was home. He could totally picture Lara in it too. She'd love what he'd done to the kitchen.

She'd probably love the playroom he'd built in the basement too. Karl hadn't missed the gleam in her eye when he'd been roping Jan, and he'd been fantasizing about binding Lara. She'd love it, he just knew it.

If he could ever get her down there. Where the hell was she? Finally, just before nine o'clock, he called her.

"Lara's phone."

Heat flashed through him. That was not Lara, that was a man. A dead man. "Who is this?"

"Who's this?"

"This is Karl. I'd like to speak with Lara please."

"Hi, Karl, this is Peter, Lara's friend. She's not here right now. Can I take a message?"

A message? Oh, no, not this time. "Where is she? I'd prefer to speak with her myself."

"She's not here, but I'll tell you where she went, after we have a quick talk."

Sounds of a short tussle and a very firm "Peter!" could be heard clearly, then a voice Karl instantly recognized came over the line. "Mr. Dawson, I'll be happy to tell you where Lara is after you tell me what you did to her."

His heart skipped a beat. "What does that mean, Graham? What happened?"

"You tell *me*. She was fine yesterday. Then today she completely avoided us, and went out to hustle pool looking like she was going out to turn tricks. Lara hasn't dressed that outrageously since she moved in here two years ago. We've worked long and hard to build a friendship, and now she's on the run emotionally."

"Damn it!" He'd been so careful to not scare her. "Where does she shoot pool?"

Graham named the pub where Karl had met her for drinks the night he'd told her he was a Dom, and hung up quickly. He was done being careful.

Peter stared at Graham in amazement. "That was . . ."

Graham did a quick pirouette in the middle of the kitchen and took a bow. "Ingenious? Brilliant? Inspired?"

"Evil," Peter said. Then he grinned. "And very inspired. But why?"

"I was there when they met, and I've seen them both almost every day since. Yesterday he was a bear, today he was unbearable." He gave a dramatic shudder. "Lara's crept up here and reached out more in the last few weeks than the last two years, but at this rate . . . I'll be pregnant before she admits she wants a happily-ever-after with him."

Peter gaped. "Pregnant?"

"Don't worry, big boy, it's just a metaphor. I'm not ready for kids." He swept through the doorway to the living room, practically dancing with glee. "Those two are perfect for each other, but they have so many walls and head issues that they're never gonna get past them until one of them stops tiptoeing around and punches through the other's wall. We both know Lara's tough, but she's no match for my boss."

Peter followed his lover, unable to take his eyes off of him. "Graham, come sit with me."

Graham sashayed across the living room, grinning. "I wish I could see what happens when he gets to the pub. Maybe we should go have a drink?"

Rolling his shoulders to release some tension, Peter sat on the edge of the sofa. His stomach was tight and his pulse was racing. This was it . . . this was the perfect time.

He reached out and snagged Graham's hand, pulling him down onto the sofa beside him.

"Graham, listen to me." He turned and cupped a hand around the back of Graham's head, his fingers massaging his lover's soft skin. "Are you still worried about me wanting Lara? Is that why you're so determined to get them together all of a sudden?"

Graham's eyes flicked away and then back. "Maybe," he admitted softly.

"I only want you. I'm sorry that my remark about sometimes wanting a female hit you so hard. I'm sorry I didn't understand what it would do to you. I'm sorry that I even considered you might get a little hysterical and slash her tires. But this has to stop. *You* are who I want. Stop worrying about her, or any other woman okay?"

Graham nodded, but Peter still saw the doubt in his eyes. And he knew how to get rid of it. He sucked in a deep breath and slid off the sofa and onto one knee. With a trembling hand he held out the little blue jewelry box that had been burning a hole in his pocket for the past month.

"Graham Nelson, will you marry me and spend the rest of your life with me, and only me?"

"Oh my God!" Graham's hands fluttered about and Peter saw pure love and happiness shine through his tears as he stared at the gold band in the box.

But he didn't reach for it.

Peter's heart stopped, then kick started again at triple the speed. He hadn't answered. Why didn't he answer?

"Graham?"

Graham folded his hands primly in his lap and met Peter's gaze. "Before I say yes, I need you to tell me, honestly and completely . . ."

"Anything," he breathed the word.

"I want only you. Can you commit to the same thing? *Only* me? Don't lie to me, or yourself, about this, Peter. Is this just your way of making up for thinking I was a crazy stalker?"

"No!" Graham's face went white and Peter scrambled to get everything out at once. "I mean, yes, only you! No, Graham, this isn't out of guilt. I bought this ring over a month ago. I just never got up the nerve to give it to you, and now seemed like the perfect time. I'm never going to let you doubt me or my commitment to you again."

"Ohhh," Visibly melting, Graham's lips parted, cheeks flushed and eyes widened as he stared at Peter. Then he snatched the ring from Peter's hands. "Then yes! Yes!"

Once the ring was on his hand, Graham launched himself off the sofa and on top of Peter, taking them both to the floor. As Graham planted kisses all over his face, Peter laughed, feeling lighthearted for the first time in way too long. "I guess this means you don't want to go have a drink at the pub anymore?"

31

Karl strode into the pub, determined to find his little runaway and make her face what was happening between them and acknowledge it. He spotted her at the pool tables right away, and the breath rushed from his body. Those black leather fuck-me boots accentuated her curvy calves and made the length of bare thigh beneath her barely there tartan skirt all the more enticing. Her upper body was completely covered, but only with a layer of sheer material that hid nothing, including the shiny black PVC push-up bra she wore.

PVC? His girl had a PVC bra that he'd never seen. That had to change.

He knew the instant she saw him coming. Her facial expression didn't change, but her stance shifted and her shoulders went back. She thought she was ready for him.

Stepping up, he put his name on the board to play the winner and went to stand at the high table a few feet away. Close enough to see and hear everything that happened at the table, but far enough away that she would have to come to him.

"What can I get you to drink?"

Karl turned his gaze on the waitress and smiled. The pretty girl's eyes widened, her cheeks flushed, and she tilted her head. "I'll have a beer, please."

"I remember you," she smiled. "And I remember what brand." With a saucy wink she left to get his drink.

"Come on, baby, you can do better than that." Lara taunted the guy she was playing with a teasing smile. "You said you were going to give me a run for my money."

"The game's not over yet, sweetness. You have to bank the eight to win."

Karl saw her eye twitch at the endearment but she hid her distaste well. "Not a problem," she said as she studied the table.

When she bent over to line up her shot, every man, punk, and stud in that corner of the room saw the matching PVC thong she wore under her skirt.

"You okay?"

He cut his eyes to the waitress standing at his table, and she stepped back. He realized he must not be hiding his emotions very well and made an effort to smile. "Sure," he said pulling a bill from his wallet. "I'm great. Keep the change."

Sudden jeering and hooting laughter erupted and the waitress grinned. "Sounds like Lara won another game. That girl's been cleaning house tonight."

"You know her?" That surprised him.

"She comes in to shoot some pool every once and while. She usually wins." She narrowed her eyes at him. "Weren't you with her last time you were here?"

He nodded. "I was, and I'll be taking her with me when I leave again tonight too."

"I've heard that before," she laughed. "But Lara's not one to go where she's already been."

So his girl was scared of relationships, but she had them all over the place. Graham and Peter obviously cared about her, the waitress knew her by name, and she'd had the same job for almost five years. There was definitely hope.

Lara avoided his gaze while the next guy racked the balls. She got ready to start the next game, but her body language couldn't hide her awareness of him. She talked and flirted with every person there, men and women alike, except him.

Which was fine. He wasn't there to flirt. He watched her play and knew he could beat her. She was good, but she played the player, not the table. He would not be distracted by her bending, flirting, and sassy attitude. He also wouldn't be playing for money.

Pride filled him when she sank the eight while the other guy still had five balls up. She *was* good.

She swept the bills up off the side of the table and tucked them into the top of her boot. Ignoring the way his cock twitched at the sight of those boots, he put down his beer and stepped up to the table. It was his turn now.

Lara stood at the head of the table, cue stick in hand, her gaze burning into his as he racked the balls. When they were set, he strode around and stood too close to her.

"I see you like to play for money," he said.

She stepped back and he saw the anger flare in her eyes. "Money is good," she said, tilting her head up.

He stepped closer, trapping her between him and the table. "I'm not interested in your money, sugar."

The fire in Karl's eyes made Lara's heart stutter. It was all she could do to string her words together in some sort of sense at his closeness. "Then what are you interested in?"

"You."

Oh God, how had he found her there? Why had he found her there? "I thought you said we weren't going to see each other until next week?"

"Are you guys going to play, or talk all night?"

The loud call made her start, and Karl turned his head slowly. She didn't need to see the look he gave the speaker; she saw the reaction to it and adrenaline shot through her. "Sorry, man. Take your time."

"I thought we were going to stay in contact," Karl said when he turned back to her.

She lifted her shoulders and let them fall. "I emailed you." It was a fight to stay casual, but she couldn't let him know how much he affected her. He already had too much power over her.

His voice was a soft purr. "One email isn't staying in contact."

Tilting her head at the table she dredged up a flirty smile and changed the subject. "What are we playing for if not money?"

He searched her eyes and her breath caught in her throat. The air between them heated and the room around them disappeared. All she could see was him, all she could smell was him. She could feel his energy reaching out and wrapping around her. He leaned in, his hands bracketing her hips against the pool table, his lips brushing against her ear as he spoke. "I'm done playing. I'm here for you."

Her chest tightened and she fought to breathe. He must've felt her nod though because he stepped back and took the pool cue from her hand. His hand at the small of her back guided her away from the table and she went.

"The table's yours," Karl said to the guy who'd backed off moments earlier, and they left the bar.

His hand burned through her thin shirt as they walked. She struggled to remember what it was she had to say to him. By the time they were in the parking lot, her head was starting to clear.

"My car," she said. "I drove."

Karl nodded. "Follow me to my house."

"But I live closer."

He arched an eyebrow and she nodded. "I'll follow you."

He walked her to her car. Once she was in, he went to his truck and she waited for him to pull out. She followed him automatically, and she was glad for that because she needed time to think.

Why she didn't think he would come looking for her when she hadn't emailed back she didn't know. She should've known. If she'd written something so . . . personal and sincere and not gotten a response, she'd have been pissed off too. Only Karl didn't really seem pissed off. More determined.

Her heart pounded. Scarily determined.

Really, he'd said everything she wanted to hear. He hadn't pressured her, just told her that talking to him, telling him what she felt was good. He was being patient and caring and confident . . . and after seeing Graham and Peter, and feeling the raw emotion in the room when they were arguing . . . then when they were making love—it was too much.

She just needed time, that was all. Time to get her feet back under her and her life back on track. Time to remember that sex was good, but she sucked at relationships.

She was surprised to see the modest bungalow-style house Karl lived in. It was nice and homey—exactly what she always wanted for herself. He opened the door for her and she stepped inside, unsure of where to go.

"Follow me," he said, and headed down the short hall.

"Wow." She stopped dead inside the kitchen. "This is beautiful."

Karl was at the fridge, a couple of water bottles in his hand. "When you cooked me dinner the other night I knew you'd love it. I had it renovated a couple of years ago."

Lara examined the dark wood cupboards, a gleaming countertop, and a center island with a sink. Her fingertips itched to pull down a shiny pot from the hanging rack and whip up a batch of homemade soup. "I've always wanted a kitchen like this," she whispered.

"It's yours."

Her jaw dropped. "What?"

"Everything I have is yours, Lara." He came toward her, his gaze intent, his movements primal and predatory. "I'm man enough to admit when I make a mistake, and trying to play it cool with you—trying to train you as a traditional submissive—was a mistake. You're not traditional. You're not like anyone I've ever met, and that's what makes you special."

"What? Wait—Karl." Lara held up a hand for him to stop. "This is too much. I don't think I can do this."

He didn't stop until he was inches from her. He braced his hands on the kitchen island behind her, boxing her in. "Do what, exactly? Talk to me, sugar."

Her chest tightened and her pulse raced. Blood rushed to her head with a roar and she put her hands on his chest to push him away, only to curl her fingers into his shirt and pull him closer. She leaned into him, burying her nose against his neck and breathing deep.

"Talk to me, Lara. Tell me what is going on inside that pretty head of yours."

"I don't know," she whispered. "You mess me up, Karl, until I don't know what I want anymore."

His jaw rubbed against the top of her head, and she wrapped her arms around his waist. His hands were still on the countertop, and she longed for the feel of them holding her.

When it became clear he wasn't going to say anything, she closed her eyes, took another deep breath, and jumped in. He went after her, he took her to *his* home, and he made it clear he wanted a relationship. She was not going to be the chicken shit and run away again.

"When I'm not with you, I can think straight and life is normal. I know that what we have is different than anything I've experienced, but I also realize that we barely know each other! Then, when I'm with you, all I want *is* you. It's like I'm hypnotized or something. I want your hands on me, your mouth on me, your cock buried deep inside me, filling me up. That's good, I can handle lust. The kink doesn't bother me, either. Whether or not I'm submissive, I have no idea, but I do know that I enjoy everything you do to me, and I fantasize about so much more. Fantasies I've never even acknowledged until I met you. I've always loved cock. I love to feel it, touch it, smell it, and taste it. My deepest fantasy would be to be surrounded by cock. Two men would be good, but three would be better, four would be . . . too many. I want to be filled at every entrance . . . I want to be fucked." She stopped. Karl's heart was pounding beneath her ear, his entire body hard in her arms.

Yet, he still said nothing.

Opening her mouth, she admitted the scariest part. "And then I want to be held and cuddled and loved."

A growl rumbled up from Karl's chest as he shifted. His arms came around her, squeezing her tight, before one hand slipped under her jaw and tilted her head back. "Look at me," he commanded.

She opened her eyes, her breath catching at the emotion she saw.

"What I want is to make you mine. I know that scares you, but you are a brave and bold and adventurous woman, and I know you won't let your fear get in the way of what you want. Even more than that, I want to give you what you need—and what we both need, to exist in a way that is true to our basic nature, is each other." He stepped back, his arms dropping to his sides, not touching her, not pressuring her. He just stood there, letting her see him, and the desire he felt so clearly. "Will you give us a chance?"

Adrenaline shot through her veins and her body flushed with heat. Her hands rose, automatically reaching for him even while her mind tried to form the right words. "Yes, but—"

"No buts allowed, Lara. You either give us a chance, or you don't."

"I want to, but I'm scared!"

Shit! She hadn't meant to say that! "Karl, I suck at relationships, I told you that. I want this, what you say sounds so good, the way you make me feel is so good, but I don't know that I can give that back to you."

He reached for her then. His hands cupped her cheeks, holding her face close as he stared deep into her eyes. Searching, seeking an answer as a rough thumb drifted across her lower lip.

"Don't you worry about that. And don't let your fear rule you. It's okay to be scared, just don't let it stop you from going after what you want. I'm not saying it will be easy, but I am saying you'll never be alone in this. I'm here for you."

He leaned in and she closed her eyes as his lips pressed against hers. Slow, soft, and oh so seductively. Strong fingers slid to the back of her head, buried in her hair, and then applied steady pressure, tightening, pulling, and tilting her head back until she couldn't move.

Everything inside her tensed, then relaxed, melting until she was mass of quivering desire, straining to be closer to him.

It hit her then, she believed him. She trusted him.

There was only one thing left for her to say. "Yes. I want it all."

32

Finally! Tension rushed from Karl's body, his knees weakened and he pressed his forehead against Lara's, leaning into her. Leaning on her.

When he'd gone after her earlier that night, he'd been scared and angry. His plan was to find her and drag her back to his place, by her hair if he had to. The whole scene had been planned in his mind. He'd tie her up and sensually tease, torture, and torment her until she admitted she wanted more than sex with him. That she felt the emotional connection and admitted that she couldn't run from it anymore. He wanted her promise she wouldn't run from him again, and he'd been ready to demand it from her.

Instead, she'd sucker punched him with her soft panicked words. She'd just given him everything he wanted without having to demand it.

Suddenly, his intense need to own was replaced by the intense need to cherish the gift she'd just given him. His arms went around her and he lowered his head. Her soft lips parted and her eager tongue welcomed him inside her.

Tongues stroked and arousal grew as he reached down and cupped her ass, lifting her against him. Her legs wrapped around his hips, her arms around his neck and he stepped forward again, settling her on the kitchen island. He reveled in the feel of her pressed against him, her legs and arms around him as he trailed kisses across her jaw to her neck and sucked on the soft flesh of her earlobe.

Her gasp of pleasure set his blood on fire and he rocked against her core. Her back arched, and her thighs tightened around his waist.

"Oh, yes," she moaned. "So good, Karl."

One quick move and he had her flimsy top over her head and on the floor. One hand splayed across her back, cradling her weight as he licked and nibbled his way across her collarbone. Her spicy vanilla scent filled his head and he unsnapped her bra. The shiny material fell away and he cupped a breast, the warm plump flesh filling the palm of his hand perfectly. Opening his mouth, he licked the rigid tip, then wrapped his lips around it and suckled gently.

She tasted so good, he sucked harder and her cry echoed through the room as she arched into him.

He pulled away and lavished attention on the other nipple. Using his tongue and teeth, he had her moaning and squirming in his arms within seconds. Kissing his way back up to her mouth, he laid her out on the countertop and slid a hand between their bodies—between her thighs.

When he encountered the slick PVC barrier, he groaned. "Do you have any idea what this underwear does to me?"

"I wore it for you," she said.

He pulled the elastic and snapped it against her skin. Then he slipped a finger under the elastic and tickled her pussy lips lightly. "You wore it for me, but you ran from me?"

"I hoped you'd—I knew you'd come after me." Her hands clutched at his back, her nails digging in as she tugged his shirt from his waistband. "Off. Take this off . . . please . . . I need to feel you . . . against me."

He got rid of his shirt and stretched out on top of her. For a minute he just pressed down. Blanketing her with his body, so her breasts fit into the curve of his chest, her legs wrapped around him. He nuzzled her neck. This was home. This was the perfect fit.

Lara shifted beneath him, her mewl of distress alerting him to the degree of her need. "Shh, baby." He brushed a lock of hair behind her ear. "I'm going to take good care of you. I promise."

Reaching beneath her skirt he stepped back and tugged her thong right off. "You're going to wear these for me again soon, sugar."

A quick flick of his wrist undid his jeans and gave his cock some room to breathe as he went down on his knees and positioned Lara's legs over his shoulders.

For a moment he just stared, he couldn't help it. Her pretty pink pussy was slick and shiny with her need and the smell made his head light. He closed his eyes and leaned in, taking one long slow lick straight up the middle. Her muscles tensed, her legs lifting as she cried out.

Eager for more of her, he used his thumbs to spread her open, and he went to work. His tongue nudged her rock-hard clit, swirled around it, flicked it, then he sealed his lips over it and sucked until her fingers dug into his skull and her body rocked against him so hard he almost fell over.

When she calmed, he started again. This time he licked around her entrance, drinking in her flavor, her scent, and the purr of contentment that he could hear so clearly.

He thrust his tongue in as deep as he could, and wiggled it around, enjoying the pliant muscles that clutched at him, trying to take him deeper. He pulled back, replacing his tongue with a finger.

Lara's hips began to roll and he matched her rhythm, fucking her with his hand while his mouth went back to the rigid button of her clit. As soon as his tongue flicked out, her hips jerked and her purr became a growl.

"That's my girl. Come for me again, baby."

He added another finger to her cunt, as he licked, sucked, and nibbled on her clit. Her thighs clenched around his head, pulling him closer and closing out everything but the feel, smell, and taste of her. He scraped his teeth over the sensitive button and felt her cunt spasm. He did it again and again until her insides were sucking at his finger and she was bucking wildly against his mouth.

When her legs were finally just lying against his shoulders again, Karl shifted back and took a deep breath. God, she was wonderful!

Standing awkwardly, he toed off his boots and shucked his jeans and underwear. When he was naked, his cock so hard it nudged against his belly for warmth, he reached for the snap on her little tartan skirt. She reached for his cock and he pushed her hand away. If she touched him then, he'd go off like a rocket. She tested his control too much.

"Lift," he said. Her hips came up and he tugged the skirt off her and stepped between her thighs again.

She reached for him again, growling when he slapped her hand away again. "No, Lara."

"Why not?" Her hands twitched and she sat up, giving him her best hurt puppy look. He shook his head and grinned at her as she waited breathlessly for his next move.

It was at that point that she finally acknowledged, with her heart and soul, that she truly didn't care what his next move was, as long as he didn't walk away. All she wanted was for him to continue to look at her, to touch her, to *want* her.

"Because," he said as he slid his arms around her and pulled her tight against him. "I'm taking you to the bedroom, and I'm going to love you until you can't walk. I can't do that if you touch me now."

Lara's heart skipped a beat. He was going to *love* her until she couldn't walk!

Karl lifted, and cradled her against him as they left the kitchen.

She didn't even bother to look around at his house. It didn't matter anymore, all that mattered was that he held her and he wasn't going to let her go. When they got to the bedroom, Karl laid her gently down on the bed and covered her body with his.

He reached out and a lamp beside the bed lit the room. "I need to see you," he said.

"I want to see you too." She cupped his cheek with her hand, the rough stubble of a day's beard growth tickling the palm. "I can't believe this is real. That you're real."

"I'm very real, baby. And I'm all yours." With no other warning, he shifted, and his cock slid home.

They didn't speak and didn't move other than to match the rhythm of their bodies as they undulated and danced as one. Lara stared deep into Karl's molten chocolate eyes and saw dreams she never even knew she had coming true. Their breathing matched, picking up speed together as Karl thrust home again and again, filling her up and claiming her at the same time.

His eyes became heavy lidded and a bead of sweat dripped from his forehead to her lip. Her tongue darted out and she tasted him, taking anything he had to give her. A groan of pleasure rumbled from his belly and his head dropped, his gaze still locked with hers as he picked up speed.

Lara arched up, locking her ankles behind his back, her gasp at the new angle the trigger that finally set him off.

"Lara," he called out, trembling in her arms as his cock swelled and throbbed and finally erupted inside her.

The warmth of his fluid filling her so deeply set off her own orgasm and waves of pleasure rolled over her, stealing the breath from her body.

When Karl collapsed on top of her, Lara wrapped her arms around him, cupped the back of his head, and stroked his hair gently. After a moment, he rolled to the side, but she kept her hold on him so that his head lay on her breast, his breath tickling her nipple as they both fell into an exhausted sleep.

33

Y ou are definitely a sexual submissive," Karl said as he held out a banana for her to bite. They were still naked, and still in bed, despite the Saturday morning sunshine trying to intrude on their coziness.

"It might go even deeper than that," he continued. "But we won't know until we explore it further."

She tried not to let her insecurity show when she swallowed and asked if it mattered.

"Does what matter? If your submissiveness goes deeper than sex?"

"Or if it doesn't."

He reached out and ran a thumb over her bottom lip, his gaze turning liquid when she opened for him and sucked on the tip. "No, sugar, it doesn't matter to me at all."

"But you do think I'm submissive? You need me to be submissive on some level." She couldn't believe she was sitting in bed with supersexy Karl Dawson and being hand-fed breakfast. Okay, so breakfast was a banana and orange slices, but it was still unbelievable.

"You make it sound like a condition of us being together, when, in reality, it's the reason why we can be together." He shifted, his expression solemn. "I don't want you to feel intimidated by the terms, Lara. They're just words, labels that really don't have any one meaning. There are as many different levels and types of Dominants and submissives as there are people. What makes someone in this lifestyle special is that they strive to know themselves. To look deep inside and acknowledge what it is they need to be happy and content."

"Yet you're labeling me a sexual submissive. What exactly does this mean, *to you*? I've read a lot on the Internet. Articles, essays, and even blogs, but really—I don't care what they say. I want to know how *you* define this."

He stared at her. "What?" she asked, smoothing a hand over her lips. "Do I have something on my face?"

"No. You just amaze me sometimes." He leaned forward and kissed her. Long, slow, and lazy until her brain started to fuzz over and she tried to crawl into his lap.

Firm hands gripped her hips and kept her where she was. "Hang on, we're talking here, and this is important because I don't want you running scared again."

"Hurry up then," she said with a lecherous grin. "You can't

expect to sit here naked for long without me wanting to lick you all over and suck on that long hard delicious cock of yours."

Delight filled her when his cheeks flushed and he shook a finger in her face. "Talking dirty will not get you what you want, my girl. Am I going to have to tie you up to continue our lessons?"

A shiver rippled through her and her nipples peaked.

Karl laughed. "Oh ho, you want to be tied up!"

"Whatever." She shrugged. "It looked like Jan enjoyed it. It could be fun."

"There's a lot Jan enjoys that you might not. Don't measure yourself by what others enjoy, Lara. Always be honest with me." He pinched her chin between his thumb and forefinger, forcing her to meet his gaze. "Promise?"

She nodded.

"Say it."

"I promise." Unable to let things get too serious she grinned at him. "And I honestly do think it could be fun."

His left eyelid dropped in a lazy wink that stirred her blood. "Oh, it will be."

They stared at one another, the air stilling, heating. Lara's heart pounded. Last night had been amazing and she was not someone who handled emotions well. She needed to tell Karl that. She cared about him, she really did, but she wasn't sure she could ever love anybody. Not like that.

Not like he deserved.

"Karl," she said softly, reaching for his hand. A knot formed in the pit of her belly, burning there like the gateway to Hell for leading this amazing man on. "Everything I've said is true. I care about you more than I thought possible, and I do want it all, but there's something you need to know."

"Okay." His hand rolled over under hers and their fingers twined together.

"I don't always handle my emotions so well. Well, aside from the sex and the pleasurable ones. But the way you make me feel, I want it all, I do, but you need to know that I'm not sure I can ever really love you. If I can ever really love anyone."

She didn't know what she expected, but it wasn't the smile he gave her. "Don't worry so much, sugar. We're on this journey together, no matter how it goes.

"I'm only going to say all this once more, so listen carefully. I sense a need in you that balances my own. The need to be dominated, to be told what to do, and to be praised for your behavior. You're very strong and independent, and I love that. I don't want or need a slave, but I do need someone who will submit to me at times. You have the need to know that someone cares enough about you to praise or punish you."

He stopped and looked at her. Instinctively Lara nodded. "Yes, Sir."

"I'm a Dom. There is something inside me that craves the submission of another. It feeds my soul to see your eagerness, to feel it, and drink it in. Nothing will please me more than to see that in your eyes, and to push you beyond even what you think you desire. We balance each other, make each other stronger, and better. But only if you accept that our relationship is just that—a relationship. The sexual aspects of your submission are our way in, but it's just the gateway to the garden. The rest is what we'll learn together."

"How can you be so sure?" She didn't want to doubt him. She didn't doubt *him*. She doubted herself.

"I see divorce every day. I see people who don't communicate, or who aren't honest with themselves, or their loved ones, just throw away a chance at happiness. I've seen so much of it that I gave up on finding my own happiness, but you've changed that. You're fearless in everything else in life, Lara. Why stop now?"

"I'm not." She reached for him again, and this time he welcomed her. "I'm not stopping, I just needed you to know where my head is."

"I know, sugar. And I'm okay with it." He kissed her, rolling on the bed until he was on top.

The hair stood up on the back of Lara's neck when she turned onto her street and saw the blue and white cop car in the driveway behind Graham's car. Tossing her sunglasses aside, she parked at the curb and shut off her car. There were no ambulances and the house looked okay, so she forced herself to take a deep breath. Then another.

Calm, Lara.

Adrenaline flooded her veins as she tried not to race up the driveway. She turned the corner to the back of the house and saw Graham and Peter standing next to a uniformed officer with a notepad in hand. They were standing by the separate entrance to her apartment.

"What's going on?" Behind them she could see someone moving around inside her place. "Peter? Graham?"

Peter waved her closer, his posture stiff, a frown creasing his forehead. "Graham went downstairs this morning to, uhmm, see how last night went for you, and found the door open. When he went inside, he saw that the bedroom was trashed."

"Next time you stay out all night, you call us!" Graham shook a finger at her.

"Graham," Peter cautioned. "We knew where she was, and who she was with. It's okay."

Graham's eyes were wide, his arms folded tight across his chest as he stared at her. He'd been worried about her. Scared for her, even! "I'm fine, Graham." She should call Karl though.

"Nothing is missing as far as we can tell, Miss Fox." The young cop—his name badge said Mathews—finally spoke up. "But you'll need to let us know for sure."

"That makes sense," she said, fighting to stay calm. "I don't have much worth stealing, just my computer or the TV. But why would someone break into my place and not steal *anything*?"

Officer Mathews held up his notepad and gave her a steady look. "I understand someone slashed the tires on your car earlier in the week?"

She shared a glance with the boys, noticing how Peter reached for Graham's hand at the question. "Yeah. We figure it was done early Wednesday morning, before anyone was awake. I was out late, and my car was fine when I got home around two in the morning, but when I left for work . . ."

"Were you with the same friend that night as last night?"

"Yes." Anger hit her hard and fast, and she bit down to keep useless venom from spewing out. She spun on her heel and stalked away, turned, and paced back. What the hell? Why the fuck was someone doing this to her?

Someone was targeting her. There was no way she could pretend this was random. They were after her, and they were doing it whenever she was with Karl.

34

The police cruiser was pulling out of the driveway just as Karl pulled up to Lara's house. When his phone rang less than an hour after she'd left him, warmth had washed over him, only to turn to ice when he'd heard the fear-tinged anger in her voice.

He noticed the scraped up doorframe on his way in that said someone had used a screwdriver or something to pop the lock. Not very sophisticated, but it did the trick. As soon as he stepped into Lara's place he heard voices in the bedroom and headed straight there.

He saw Lara and the breath he hadn't known he was holding whooshed from him. A little light-headed, he just took in the sight of her, still dressed in her boots, skirt, and the black t-shirt of his that she'd borrowed, standing in the middle of a disaster zone.

Clothes were strewn about the room, the curtains torn off the window, the mattress half-off the bed . . . and the mirror on her dresser broken.

She had her back to the door. Graham stood on one side of her and another guy, with his arm around her shoulders, on the other.

"Lara."

All three heads spun in his direction, but Karl only saw her big blue eyes, round and full of fire. His girl was pissed *off*!

"You okay?" He wanted to go to her, but the tightly leashed anger seemed to almost be directed at him, so he waited. If she needed someone to yell at, he was there for her.

"I'm fine, thanks. But I have a few questions for you."

"We'll be upstairs if you need us, hon." The scruffy guy squeezed her shoulder and both men headed for the door. When Graham passed him, he stopped and looked Karl in the eyes.

"She's scared, she just won't admit it." He'd spoken for Karl's ears only and Karl heard him loud and clear. He also understood the unspoken warning in his assistant's gaze.

If it came down to it, Graham was on Lara's side, no matter who his boss was.

Karl walked toward Lara, tuning out the room around them, his focus totally and completely on her. Her pupils were dilated, her cheeks were flushed, and the pulse at her throat was rapid. She was strong, and she was scared, and she was using her anger to control the fear.

He didn't want her to control it. He wanted her to release it, to give it to him, to trust him to take it, and still be there for her.

"What happened?"

"Someone broke in while I was with you last night and trashed my stuff." She planted her fists on her hips and tilted her head. "Nothing was stolen, the rest of the suite wasn't even touched, just the bedroom. Just my clothes, and the bed . . . torn apart as if someone were in a jealous rage."

So that was the way her mind was coping. "And you think it has something to do with me."

"You never did tell me how many subs you have."

"You are the only anything I have."

She snorted, throwing her hands up and turning away from him.

"Lara," he snapped. "Don't turn away from me."

She faced him again, her mouth twisted and arms folded across her chest. "What about Jan?"

"Jan isn't capable of something like this. Even if she was, she and I were play partners only. Neither of us ever wanted it to be more than that."

Unease tightened his gut. *Marie might be, though.*

"And your other play partners?" She arched an eyebrow at him. "Two times in the last week something bad has happened to me, and both times, they were when I was with you. You're the connection, Karl."

"I've had many play partners over the years, Lara. Two that were regulars for the last year or so, both of whom I've spoken to and cut things off with since I met you."

"Did you make them feel as special as you made me feel? Did they think they could *have it all* with you too?"

He stepped closer, speaking softly and holding her gaze. "I never even went on a date with any of them. It was play and that was it. Until you, I'd given up on ever finding someone I could have it all with. Someone who would challenge me mentally, psychologically, and physically."

Eyes wide, she stepped back, shaking her head, and pulling her hands out of his reach.

"Stop it, Lara! Look at me. Listen to me." He grabbed her hands and pulled her against his body, pinning her hands behind her back. "Do not let this undo everything we achieved last night. These attacks are not about you and me. You've done nothing wrong and I've done nothing wrong."

She didn't struggle against him, but she didn't give in either. He pressed his forehead against hers, and willed her to look past his eyes and into his soul. "Don't use this as an excuse to run from us, Lara."

He watched and waited while she battled her inner demons, knowing only she could do it. Slowly, the tension left her body and he had his girl back. He pressed his lips against hers, elated at the way she softened and opened for him instantly. Her body melted against his, her softness blending into his hardness and they were one. No thoughts, no fears, no anger, just the comfort of two halves becoming one.

He ended the kiss slowly, not wanting to stop, but knowing they had things to deal with. Together.

Releasing her hands he gave her a small smack on the backside. "C'mon, sugar, grab a few things and come stay at my place for a few days."

"Why?" Her brow puckered.

"Your door is messed up and probably can't be fixed until Monday, so it's not safe here until we figure out what's going on." He did not want her alone in that suite again. Not until they caught whoever was stalking her. Maybe not ever.

Her back went up and her chin went out. "I don't need a big strong man to protect me."

"I know you don't, sugar. This is for me, not you."

Karl saw the indecision in her eyes. She wanted to stay independent, but she wanted to be with him too, and he wasn't above using that. Reaching out he wrapped his arms around her and pulled her close in a hug. Bending his head, he whispered in her ear. "If you come stay with me, I'll tie you up."

Her eyes lit up and she grinned. "Oh, okay then. You convinced me."

The knot in his chest easing, he kissed her again, and then stepped back. "You gather some things. I'll go tell Graham you'll be with me."

Graham's body heat warmed Peter's back as he watched Lara's car turn down the road and follow Karl Dawson's truck away from their home.

"What are you thinking?"

Peter turned from the window to face his boy. "Just how glad I am that Lara wasn't home last night. And that she's finally letting someone close enough to stand by her."

Graham shook his head. "I've never seen him like that, Peter. And I've seen him angry enough that just looking at him made my knees knock. But that . . . that was cold fury. I would not want to be the person on the receiving end of that."

Karl had come upstairs and introduced himself to Peter, asked for Lara's phone and given them all his contact numbers. "Lara's going to stay with me for the rest of the weekend, longer if I can convince her, but that will give you time to get the door repaired." The tightly leashed fury had left his voice when he'd looked at the men and actually thanked them for being such good friends to Lara.

Peter smiled at him. "I'm glad. It's obvious he loves her. And that he understands her."

Graham cuddled up to Peter, his arms going around his waist and Peter's heart swelled, filling with love. "Everyone needs someone," he said simply. "I'm so glad I have you."

35

The weekend at Karl's flew by. When Lara finished work on Monday she went back to her own place to find the doorframe fixed and a nice new shiny deadbolt installed. So she decided to stay home. She could tell by Karl's tone of voice when she called him that he didn't care if the door was fixed—he wanted her back at his place. But he didn't order her there, or even ask.

Instead, he said, "You know where I am, and feel free to use your key anytime."

Lara hung up the phone and dropped onto her sofa with a dreamy smile in place. He understood. He understood her need to stand on her own, and yet he made sure she knew she didn't have to. She hugged the throw pillow to her chest and drifted off to sleep.

"Do you think she's dead?"

A finger poked her shoulder roughly, and she growled. "I'm awake now. What do you want?"

"Dinner and a movie," Graham said.

Lara opened her eyes and sat up on the sofa. He didn't have dinner, or a movie, in his hands. Instead he stood there, left hand extended, palm down.

"What?" Then she saw it and she jumped up from the sofa. "Oh my God! You guys are getting married?"

Peter turned away from his spot by her window, his cheeks flushed, his pride obvious as he watched Graham show off his ring.

She gave Graham a big hug and pulled back to admire the ring. "Very nice. I'm so happy for you."

"Good," Graham said. "Now that you know all about our love life, tell us about yours."

Heat crept up her neck and she glanced over at Peter, who had moved on to her second window with a long wooden stick in his hand. "What are you doing?"

"I have a guy coming tomorrow to install bars on these windows, but for tonight, these will have to do." He placed the wooden dowel in the bottom of the window frame so that it couldn't be slid open.

"No one's going to break in tonight. Don't worry."

Peter looked at her. "You know who it is?"

"Not yet, but they've yet to attack *me*. They only go after my things, so I think I'm okay for a while longer." She twisted her hands and sat down on the sofa again. "I think it's one of Karl's old playmates."

"Playmates?"

Oops. "Girlfriends, whatever." She waved a hand.

"It's okay, Lara. We know he's a Dom."

Eyes wide, she stared at them, unable to think of something to say. If they knew he was a Dom, they'd have to know she let him top her.

Peter dropped onto the sofa next to her and reached for her hand. "Those of us who play in that lifestyle tend to recognize it in others that we meet."

She looked at Graham, who'd settled down in the chair across from them. "You knew all along? And you didn't warn me!"

He held up his hands. "Hey, I tried to tell you dating him might not be the smartest move."

True, but she hadn't listened. Thank God.

Wait a minute. "Those of you who play in the lifestyle?" Now it all made sense. The intense energy that sometimes sprung up from nowhere when the two of them were around. The way Peter always seemed to be able to calm Graham down or shut him up with a word.

She smacked herself in the forehead. "How did I not see that?"

The boys chuckled and she shook her head. She'd been blind.

"We don't hide it, but we don't advertise our private life either. It's for us, and us only. Just like yours is for you."

"So you don't think it's weird? For me, I mean, to all

of a sudden enjoy having someone tell me what—control—dominate?" She threw up her hand and flopped back against the cushions. "See! None of those really apply! Karl doesn't dominate me, or tell me what to do, or even try to control me. Not really."

Peter laid a warm hand on her shoulder. "He guides you. He leads and you follow, but it's where you want to go, right?"

"Yeah, that makes sense. He leads. Sometimes with a bit more arrogance than others—but he leads. He'd never force me to do anything."

"A good Dom won't." Peter smiled at her. "You realize it's probably killing him to let you stay here alone tonight?"

She nodded. "I know. But I have to. I have to prove to myself that I'm still me, and not just his girl."

The boys stood. "Okay then, we're going to leave you alone, but we'll be upstairs, the door's open, as always."

Peter hugged her, then Graham, and she thanked them. "I'll be fine, but it's nice to know you're there for me."

"Always, honey!" Graham blew her a kiss from the stairs up to their place.

Her stomach rumbled and she made herself a peanut butter sandwich, thinking about how nice it was to have friends. And they were friends. She'd never though of the boys as anything more than housemates until recently, but they'd proven they were so much more than that.

When she stepped inside her bedroom and saw that the clothes that could be salvaged were hanging in her closet, the curtains were rehung, and the bed made up with a new coverlet, she couldn't fight the tears anymore.

How did she get so lucky to have found such good friends?

The following Monday morning Karl had just settled in at his desk with a steaming mug of coffee when his email program pinged. Monday morning hell was starting early. He opened the window and saw that the email was from Lara, and warmth spread through him.

Sure it had only been one week since they'd really committed to each other, but he knew it was going to last—they were going to last.

He'd stressed a bit when she'd insisted on leaving his place last Monday, to go back to her own bed, but it had been good for them. They'd had dinner together on Wednesday and a movie on Thursday, and then on Friday, she'd automatically come back home to him for the weekend. He hadn't even needed to ask, or try to bribe her.

He still worried about her at home alone, but Graham had told him they'd had the windows barred and they were all being vigilant. The fact that he and Lara had been on two more dates and nothing had happened either night had taken the steam out of the argument that he was the cause for the attacks.

The phone in the outer office rang but Karl ignored it. Graham wasn't there yet, and his office hours didn't start for at least thirty more minutes. If it were a friend, they'd call his cell. In-

Sasha White

stead, he leaned back in his chair and clicked on the icon for Lara's email.

I just wanted you to know I was thinking of you, of your cock. Of the way my knees were still tender after I left your house because I spent so much time on them. Enjoyable time, I loved every minute that you were in my mouth. The sloppiness, your hardness, your hands in my hair, and my tongue on you. I do want more. More of that, and everything else you have to give.

Desire infused his blood and he let his head fall back, closing his eyes. His girl definitely knew how to hit him where it counted. He remembered their play the night before and his cock filled. His hand went to the cell phone on his hip, then stilled. If he called her now, he'd have to take cock in hand and deal with things there and then, and that didn't have much appeal when he really wanted her.

Instead, a new scene started playing out in his mind. Five minutes later he sat up, hit reply, and started typing.

Such a nice girl to start my day off like that, thank you. Tomorrow night, you and I are going out. I have plans. The Dungeon. Wear your boots and the PVC lingerie.

It was short and to the point. And it would drive her imagination wild.

Karl chuckled and hit send just as the phone rang again. This time Graham answered and buzzed him. "Lisa Pollack is on line one, Mr. Dawson. Are you in?"

"I'll take it," he responded, and then picked up the phone. "Lisa, how are you this morning?"

"Wonderful, Karl. Just wonderful." Her voice grated on his nerves, but he knew what was coming and he wanted that information.

"Glad to hear it. What can I do for you today?"

"It's not what you can do for me, but what I have for you. My first check showed up with all six months of back alimony, so I'm doing as I promised. You wanted my investigator's name?"

"Yes, That would be helpful."

"Marie Agnew. A lovely police officer who moonlights as an investigator. She works by referral only, so if you have a problem with her, just tell her I gave you her name."

Karl thanked her automatically and hung up the phone.

Marie.

His hands clenched into fists as puzzle pieces started to fall into place. Without thinking twice he picked up the phone and dialed Mason Hardin's private number.

When Karl had called Val to see if he could help him get ahold of the man through the club owners' network, Val had told him Mason Hardin was not a man to be fucked with. And coming from Val, that was a serious warning. But Karl felt no compunction whatsoever turning Marie over to him. Not just for taking those photos, but because there was a damn good chance she was the one harassing Lara. If he'd had any solid proof of that, he'd deal with her himself.

When a deep male voice came on the line, Karl spoke firmly. "Mason, it's Karl Dawson. I have a name for you."

"Good. I've already gone over my staff thoroughly and come up empty. I do not like the idea of someone getting away with breaking my rules and harassing my club members."

"Marie Agnew. She's not one of your staff, she's a member—and a city cop who's sidelining as a P.I."

"Well, that makes things a little more difficult. Not impossible, but difficult."

"I'll leave it to you then." Karl said his good-byes and hung up with a clear conscience. With Marie being a cop, Hardin would be an idiot to do harm to her. The man was smart enough to find another way to make his point. And Karl knew that being banned from the club and any other BDSM one in the city would be a small part of it.

Which meant he and Lara could have a very good time there the next night, with no worries.

36

Lara heard him coming before she saw him. Peeking through the new bars that protected the basement suite's windows, she saw the big black hog head up the road and roll to a stop in front of her house.

Karl turned the bike off and then stood, removing his helmet so that the last rays of sun glinted of his blond waves. The smooth movement of his body as he hung his helmet on the handlebar and twisted to take something out of the saddlebag, had her remembering just how well that body moved. Heat climbed from the knot of arousal in her belly to her chest and up her neck until her cheeks were on fire. He was so yummy she could barely stand it.

And he was all hers.

Pleasure so deep and profound that it was almost magical

filled her. Her life might have started off rough, but somewhere along the way she'd done something to please the Karma gods.

When Karl's heavy footsteps went past her window she dashed through the small suite to the door. She was eager to go, and she didn't feel the need to hide it.

She was waiting in the open doorway when he came around the corner. "Hey there, sexy."

"Hello, sugar. You're looking more sweet than sassy tonight." Stepping into the suite he crowded her until she had her back against the wall. Head tilted, his gaze drifted up her body. His hand followed, skimming up from her hip over her belly. The palm of his hand brushed her already rigid nipple then laid flat against the top of her chest.

His eyes met hers as his hand crept up, then circled her neck, pinning her to the wall. His grip wasn't tight enough to hurt, just enough to heighten her awareness and bring her complete focus onto him.

The rough pad of his thumb scraped against her sensitized skin, tilting her chin up as he lowered his head. His mouth came down on hers with such masterly intent that Lara could do nothing but luxuriate in the moment. When he stepped back, his hand dropping back to his side, she was completely boneless. Only the wall behind her kept her on her feet.

The small smile Karl wore when he held up a leather jacket said he knew exactly what his kiss had done to her. "Stand up, sugar, so I can put this on you."

With effort, she locked her knees and pushed away from the

wall. One step forward and he slid the sleeves up her arms and settled it on her shoulders. It was then that she realized it was a perfect fit.

Her fingertips pinched the pliable leather and she looked down as he zipped it up for her. Over the left breast a word was embroidered. The black on black made it subtle, but Lara could clearly see her name. "For me? You bought this just for me?"

"Of course," he said. "You're going to need something strong and warm to wear when you ride with me. Plus, you in leather was something I couldn't resist."

She just stared. Emotions she couldn't name swirled around inside her and her mouth went dry. As if he knew exactly what was happening to her, Karl grabbed her hand, kissed her cheek, and led her out the door. "Time to go, sugar. We have one stop to make before we get to The Dungeon."

Swallowing hard, Lara gave her head a shake and followed where Karl led. She stood still for him while he put a helmet over her head and secured it beneath her chin. She swung a leg over the bike and flashed Karl her thong when she noticed him staring at her bare thighs.

"Sassy girl," he growled then climbed on in front of her. He reached back, grabbed her thighs, and tugged her forward until she was flush against him. "Between the boots, the jacket, and me, you should be warm enough. Just stay close and I'll be a wind barrier for you."

He slid his helmet and sunglasses on and then started the bike. Vibrations rumbled straight through her and Lara moaned.

She shifted forward a bit, arching her back and pressing down on the seat.

Oh lord, the ride was going to be deliciously naughty.

"Lara." Karl turned his head and spoke clearly. "You are *not* allowed to come."

He revved the engine and the bike shook beneath her as he eased from the curb. *Oh shit!* It was going to be a long ride.

Lara didn't bother watching the scenery pass her by, she just snuggled up against Karl, and held on to him. She rested her head against his back, closed her eyes, and concentrated on her breathing. The vibrations from the big bike between her thighs revved and receded with irregularity, keeping her body on edge the whole time, while her mind hazed over.

By the time the bike rolled to a stop in a small back alley parking lot, Lara was almost mindless with lust.

Karl climbed off the bike and removed his helmet and glasses before going to work on hers. The second his warm fingers touched her skin, her lips parted and a soft moan came out. She stared up at him, unable to stop from rocking against the seat of the bike in tiny motions.

"Oh, sugar," he murmured, stroking his thumb over her lip. "Was that too much for you?"

She opened her mouth and sucked on his thumb. So salty and rough against her tongue. She closed her eyes and leaned into him, her hands reaching for his hips. He wrapped one arm around her shoulders, pulling her against him while his other hand slid under her skirt.

She moaned at the feel of skin against skin and rocked against his hand. "Shhhh," he murmured, pressing his chin against the top of her head. He moved her thong aside and slid two fingers inside of her.

Another moan escaped and his hand cupped the back of her head, turning it so her face was buried against his chest, hidden behind the lapel of his leather jacket. He thrust his hand against her once, twice, three times then pulled his fingers out and pinched her clit—hard. Her mouth opened and a scream of pleasure erupted, cut off when he tightened his grip on her head and she bit into his chest.

When she came back to earth, his chest was shaking. She looked up at him, worried he was mad, only to see him trying hard not to laugh.

Before she could think she balled up a fist and punched him in the gut. "Don't laugh at me!"

He took a couple of steps back and held his hands up in surrender. "I'm sorry, sugar. That was just too beautiful."

She quickly adjusted her underwear and climbed off the bike. "That was mean."

"It wasn't meant to be. I didn't realize you were so primed." He arched a silky blond brow. "Maybe I should make sure that instead of *not* masturbating when I'm not around, that you do it every time before we go for a ride."

"Or maybe not. That could be fun too."

Lara lips twitched. Okay, so there was a bit of humor to be had there. "Where are we, anyway?"

"Back entrance of Risqué nightclub. I want you to meet a couple of friends of mine."

She started to look around. "In the alley?"

A dark shape dashed out from behind a van five feet away. "Slut! Devil's whore!"

Before she knew what was happening, rough hands grabbed at Lara, pulling her almost off her feet. A strong arm wrapped around her neck and held her against a barrel chest. "You think you're too good for my brother. You think you're so damn perfect. You're just a slut. A whore who spreads her legs for the devil!"

Adrenaline kicked in full force when Lara heard the words and saw the deadly curved knife in her attacker's hand, aimed at her solar plexus.

"Hey!" Karl shouted, inching closer. "I'm the devil you want. Let her go and come after me like a man."

Hot breath coated her cheek as the guy kept ranting. "You'd rather let this devil play between your thighs than smile at my brother. Day after day, I pray for you. I've tried to warn you, but you wouldn't listen. Now it's time for you to leave him."

"Hey, asshole! Look at me. You don't want to hurt her. You like her, remember? You want me. Come on, come get me."

Lara watched Karl inch closer, his eyes on her attacker the whole time. Calm, intent, deadly.

When the arm moved and the knife pointed straight at Karl, fear spurred Lara on and she reacted instinctively.

She drove her elbow into her attacker's gut and her foot

down on his instep. The grip around her throat loosened, and she slammed her fist down and into his balls. He stumbled back and she jumped to the side as Karl tackled him and took him to the ground.

They struggled, rolling around as Lara stepped closer. Karl pinned the hand with the knife and she kicked at it. The knife skittered across the asphalt and she ran to the door of the club. She wasn't worried about Karl so much when the knife wasn't in play.

Lara banged a fist on the metal door of the club, and yanked it open. "Help! Someone call nine-one-one." Two men came running down the hallway. Heart in her throat, she turned back to the fight.

The fight was over though. Karl was coming toward her, the unconscious form of her attacker on the ground behind him. She rushed to him, wrapping her arms around him so tight she was never going to let go.

"You okay?" he asked as he tilted her chin up to look into her face.

"I'm fine. It's you that scared me to death!" She stepped back and smacked him in the shoulder. "Why did you attack him? Why didn't you just turn around and get help? Why didn't you use your fucking cell phone? Damn it, Karl, you scared the shit out of me!"

He reached out and pulled her struggling form against him. "Shhh, it's okay. We're okay."

An amused voice cut through the pounding in her ears. "I take it that's Lara?"

"Yes, this is my girl. Who, by the way, kicked ass."

She laughed against his chest, recovering quickly now that she could feel his warmth against her. "Actually, it was his instep I kicked, but I did nail him in the balls."

"You did good, sugar." Karl's arms tightened around her once more, before relaxing enough that she could step back.

"We've got Sandra Bullock to thank for that little bit of self-defense," she said with a chuckle as she looked into Karl's eyes. "Me and the boys watched *Miss Congeniality* the other night, and they made me practice the SING method. And while it didn't work exactly as planned, they'll be thrilled to know it did work!"

Karl's eyes widened slightly. "SING method?"

"Solar plexus, instep, nose, and groin."

"Crazy," he muttered and hugged her tightly once more before she pulled back. She didn't go far, though. She stayed glued to his side, one arm around his waist, and turned to meet his friend.

"Hi," she said to the tall, dark, and handsome guy.

He held out a hand, his smile big and welcoming. "Hi, Lara. I'm Valentine Ward, Karl's buddy."

A siren came from the distance, and they all looked down the alley. Two big guys from the club had her attacker rolled over, his hands tied with rope. They were trying to stand him up. "Just leave him on the ground, guys. The cops will be here in a second."

Karl walked her over, and Val followed. "Do you know him?"

A shiver ripped through her. "It's Robert. I don't know his last name, Yardley or Hadley or something. He and his brother own the garage on Hastings that I deliver parts to." She met Karl's gaze. "He always gave me the creeps."

"Good instincts."

Two cruisers turned down the alley and came to a stop nearby. The cops took Robert away, and Val and his guys went back into the club while Karl and Lara gave separate statements. It went quickly because one of the responding officers was Mathews, who'd been on the scene when her bedroom had been trashed.

Forty-five minutes later, they entered the back hallway of Risqué and Karl pinned her to the wall again.

"Before we go in there, I have to tell you something," he said. His body pressed against hers, his eyes roving over her as he brushed hair back from her face.

"I have something to say too," she whispered.

They looked at each other, eyes roaming, their breath blending, emotions completely bared. Her heart pounded in her chest, but not from fear. For the first time she could remember, Lara's heart was completely open and she wasn't afraid.

Karl opened his mouth to speak, but Lara stopped him with a finger pressed against his lips. "Let me go first," she said.

Eyes shining with love, he nodded and closed his mouth. But he didn't move away from her, and for that she was grateful. He hadn't backed down, and he hadn't let her run, and that was the way she wanted it to always be.

"Right from the start, you challenged me. At first, I thought the challenge was just your way to get me to have dinner with you, but it was more than that. You challenged me to find myself and to accept myself. And more than that, you challenged me to accept you and what you could give me."

She swallowed the lump in her throat and cupped his cheek. Her thumb smoothed over the scar running through his eyebrow, and she smiled into his glittering eyes. "You seemed to instinctively know what I needed, and you've given me more than I've ever imagined."

"You've—"

"Shush. I'm not done." She tilted her head and kissed him tenderly before continuing. "I need you to know that I understand what you've been saying. We fit. And when you tackled Robert, my heart about stopped. I don't think—I *know* no man but you could have ever convinced me that love can really be mine, but you did it and now I'm yours, Karl Dawson. But don't you ever forget that this works both ways. *You're mine too.*"

Karl's grip on her tightened, and she saw his throat working up and down as he gazed at her adoringly. "I'm yours too," he said, lowering his head and placing his lips against hers. "Forever."